閱讀經典，成為更好的自己。

愛　經　典

生
如
夏
花

泰 戈 爾 經 典 詩 選

Stray Birds &

The Crescent Moon

RABINDRANATH TAGORE

拉賓德拉納特·泰戈爾 ————著

鄭振鐸 ————————譯

緣起

愛
經
典

　　卡爾維諾說：「『經典』即是具影響力的作品，在我們的想像中留下痕跡，並藏在潛意識中。正因『經典』有這種影響力，我們更要撥時間閱讀，接受『經典』為我們帶來的改變。」因為經典作品具有這樣無窮的魅力，時報出版公司特別引進大星文化公司的「作家榜經典文庫」，期能為臺灣的經典閱讀提供另一選擇。

　　作家榜經典文庫從二〇一七年起至今，已出版超過六十本，迅速累積良好口碑，不斷榮登豆瓣讀書暢銷榜。本書系的作者都經過時代淬鍊，其作品雋永，意義深遠；所選擇的譯者，多為優秀的詩人、作家，因此譯文流暢，讀來如同原創作品般通順，沒有隔閡；而且時報在臺推出時，每部作品皆以精裝裝幀，質感更佳，是讀者想要閱讀與收藏經典時的首選。

　　現在開始讀經典，成為更好的自己。

目
次

飛鳥集 Stray Birds

新月集 The Crescent Moon

飛鳥集

Stray Birds

《飛鳥集》充溢著對人和自然的愛 [1]

　　近來小詩十分發達。它們的作者大半都是直接或間接受太戈爾 [2] 此集的影響的。此集的介紹，對於沒有機會得讀原文的，至少總有些貢獻。

　　這詩集的一部分譯稿是積了許多時候的，但大部分卻都是在西湖俞樓譯的。我在此謝謝葉聖陶、徐玉諾二君。他們替我很仔細地校讀過這部譯文，並且提供了許多重要的意見給我。

鄭振鐸
一九二二年六月二十六日

　　我譯太戈爾的《飛鳥集》是在一九二二年夏天，離現在已經有三十多個年頭了。這部《飛鳥集》共有短詩三百二十六首。我那時候只選譯了其中為自己所喜歡的和能夠懂得的若干篇。有些不太瞭解或覺得宗教的意味太濃厚的，就都刪去不譯。但也譯得不少，共譯了二百五十七首，占全部的四分之三以上，就印成一本小小的書出版。當時姚茫父先生見之，大為讚賞，便把我的譯文改用五言詩寫過，也印了出來。他的譯本是更具有中國詩的風味了。

　　現在，趁這個再版的機會，重新把我的譯本讀過幾遍，自己發現有些詩譯得不太好，甚至，有些譯錯的地方，便都把它們改正過來，同時，又把那時候沒有譯出的六十九首詩，補譯出來。現在這個樣子的新版，算是《飛鳥集》的第一次全譯本了。

太戈爾的這些短詩，看來並不難譯，但往往在短短的幾句詩裡，包涵著深邃的大道理，或尖銳的諷刺語，要譯得恰如其意，是不大容易的。它們像山坡草地上的一叢叢野花，在早晨的太陽光下，紛紛地伸出頭來。隨你喜愛什麼吧，那顏色和香味是多種多樣的。像：

> 「謝謝神，我不是一個權力的輪子，而是被壓在這輪子下的活人之一。」
> 「人類的歷史默默忍耐地等待著受辱者的勝利。」

那些詩，是帶著很深刻的譏嘲，甚至很大的悲憤的，更多的詩是充溢著對人和自然的愛的，還有些詩是像「格言」的，其中有不少是會令人諷吟有得的。又，我原來根據的本子共有三百二十六首詩，其中有一首詩與第九十八首詞句完全相同，應刪去，成為三百二十五首。英譯本的一個本子也是三百二十五首。特此聲明。

鄭振鐸
一九五六年三月十二日於北京

---

1 本書序言標題均為編者所加。
2 太戈爾即泰戈爾，文中人名及部分詞彙尊重譯者，保留原譯，未加修改，全書亦如是。

13

1 /

夏天的飛鳥，飛到我窗前唱歌，又飛去了。
秋天的黃葉，它們沒有什麼可唱，只歎息一聲，飛落在那裡。

Stray birds of summer come to my window to sing and fly away.
And yellow leaves of autumn, which have no songs, flutter and fall there with a sigh.

2 /

世界上的一隊小小的漂泊者呀，請留下你們的足印在我的文字裡。

O troupe of little vagrants of the world, leave your footprints in my words.

3 /

是大地的淚點，使她的微笑保持著青春不謝。

It is the tears of the earth that keep her smiles in bloom.

4 /

無垠的沙漠熱烈追求一葉綠草的愛，她搖搖頭笑著
飛開了。

The mighty desert is burning for the love of a blade of grass
who shakes her head and laughs and flies away.

5 /

有些看不見的手指，如懶懶的微颸似的，正在我的
心上奏著潺湲的樂聲。

Some unseen fingers, like an idle breeze, are playing upon my
heart the music of the ripples.

6 /

靜靜地聽，我的心呀，聽那世界的低語，這是它對
你求愛的表示呀。

Listen, my heart, to the whispers of the world with which it
makes love to you.

7 /

啊，美呀，在愛中找你自己吧，不要到你鏡子的諂諛中去找尋。

O Beauty, find thyself in love, not in the flattery of thy mirror.

8 /

我今晨坐在窗前，世界如一個路人似的，停留了一會，向我點點頭又走過去了。

I sit at my window this morning where the world like a passer-by stops for a moment, nods to me and goes.

9 /

人是一個初生的孩子，他的力量，就是生長的力量。

Man is a born child, his power is the power of growth.

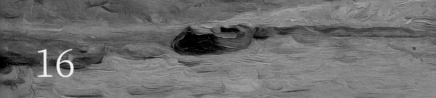

10 /

世界對著它的愛人，把它浩瀚的面具揭下了。
它變小了，小如一首歌，小如一回永恆的接吻。
The world puts off its mask of vastness to its lover.
It becomes small as one song, as one kiss of the eternal.

11 /

跳舞著的流水呀，在你途中的泥沙，要求你的歌
聲，你的流動呢。你肯挾跛足的泥沙而俱下麼？
The sands in your way beg for your song and your movement,
dancing water. Will you carry the burden of their lameness?

12 /

她的熱切的臉，如夜雨似的，攪擾著我的夢魂。
Her wishful face haunts my dreams like the rain at night.

13 /

有一次，我們夢見大家都是不相識的。
我們醒了，卻知道我們原是相親相愛的。

Once we dreamt that we were strangers.
We wake up to find that we were dear to each other.

14 /

憂思在我的心裡平靜下去，正如暮色降臨在寂靜的
山林中。

Sorrow is hushed into peace in my heart like the evening
among the silent trees.

15 /

如果你因失去了太陽而流淚，那麼你也將失去群星
了。

If you shed tears when you miss the sun, you also miss the
stars.

16 /

「海水呀，你說的是什麼？」「是永恆的疑問。」
「天空呀，你回答的話是什麼？」「是永恆的沉默。」
"What language is thine, O sea?"
"The language of eternal question."
"What language is thy answer, O sky?"
"The language of eternal silence."

17 /

創造的神祕，有如夜間的黑暗——是偉大的。而知
識的幻影卻不過如晨間之霧。
The mystery of creation is like the darkness of night —
it is great. Delusions of knowledge are like the fog of the
morning.

18 /

那些把燈背在背上的人，把他們的影子投到了自己
前面。
They throw their shadows before them who carry their
lantern on their back.

19 /

這些微颸，是樹葉的簌簌之聲呀；它們在我的心裡歡悅地微語著。

These little thoughts are the rustle of leaves; they have their whisper of joy in my mind.

20 /

主呀，我的那些願望真是愚傻呀，它們雜在祢的歌聲中喧叫著呢。

讓我只是靜聽著吧。

My wishes are fools, they shout across thy songs, my Master. Let me but listen.

21 /

光明如一個裸體的孩子，快快活活地在綠葉當中遊戲，它不知道人是會欺詐的。

The light that plays, like a naked child, among the green leaves happily knows not that man can lie.

22 /

「我們蕭蕭的樹葉都有聲響回答那暴風雨，但你是
誰呢，那樣地沉默著？」
「我不過是一朵花。」

"We, the rustling leaves, have a voice that answers the storms, but who are you so silent?"

"I am a mere flower."

23 /

神希望我們因為祂送給我們的花朵而酬答祂，而非
因為太陽和土地。

God expects answers for the flowers he sends us, not for the sun and the earth.

24 /

我的心把她的波浪在世界的海岸上沖激著，以熱淚
在上邊寫著她的題記：「我愛你。」

My heart beats her waves at the shore of the world and writes upon it her signature in tears with the words, "I love thee."

25 /

我不能選擇那最好的。
是那最好的選擇我。

I cannot choose the best.
The best chooses me.

26 /

女人啊，你在料理家務的時候，你的手腳歌唱著，
正如山間的溪水歌唱著在小石中流過。

Woman, when you move about in your household service
your limbs sing like a hill stream among its pebbles.

27 /

我說不出這心為什麼那樣默默地頹喪著。
是為了它那不曾要求，不曾知道，不曾記得的小小
的需要。

I cannot tell why this heart languishes in silence.
It is for small needs it never asks, or knows or remembers.

28 /

「月兒呀，你在等候什麼呢？」
「向我將讓位給他的太陽致敬。」
"Moon, for what do you wait?"
"To salute the sun for whom I must make way."

29 /

不要因為峭壁是高的，便讓你的愛情坐在峭壁上。
Do not seat your love upon a precipice because it is high.

30 /

生命從世界得到資產，愛情使它得到價值。
Life finds its wealth by the claims of the world, and its worth by the claims of love.

31 /

休息與工作的關係，正如眼瞼與眼睛的關係。

Rest belongs to the work as the eyelids to the eyes.

32 /

我存在，乃是所謂生命的一個永久的奇蹟。

That I exist is a perpetual surprise which is life.

33 /

瀑布歌唱道：「我得到自由時便有了歌聲了。」

The waterfall sings, "I find my song, when I find my freedom."

34 /

玻璃燈因為瓦燈叫它作表兄而責備瓦燈。但當明
月出來時，玻璃燈卻溫和地微笑著，叫明月為——
「我親愛的，親愛的姊姊。」

While the glass lamp rebukes the earthen for calling it cousin,
the moon rises, and the glass lamp, with a bland smile, calls
her, "My dear, dear sister."

35 /

綠樹長到了我的窗前，彷彿是喑啞的大地發出的渴
望的聲音。

The trees come up to my window like the yearning voice of
the dumb earth.

36 /

群星不怕顯得像螢火蟲那樣。

The stars are not afraid to appear like fireflies.

37　/

他把他的刀劍當作他的上帝。
當他的刀劍勝利時他自己卻失敗了。

He has made his weapons his gods.
When his weapons win he is defeated himself.

38　/

世界在躊躇之心的琴弦上跑過去，奏出憂鬱的樂聲。

The world rushes on over the strings of the lingering heart
making the music of sadness.

39　/

「陰影」戴上她的面紗，祕密地，溫順地，用她的
沉默的愛的腳步，跟在「光」後面。

Shadow, with her veil drawn, follows Light in secret
meekness, with her silent steps of love.

40 /

鳥兒願為一朵雲。
雲兒願為一隻鳥。

The bird wishes it were a cloud.
The cloud wishes it were a bird.

41 /

我們如海鷗之與波濤相遇似的，遇見了，走近了。
海鷗飛去，波濤滾滾地流開，我們也分別了。

Like the meeting of the seagulls and the waves we meet and
come near. The seagulls fly off, the waves roll away and we
depart.

42 /

當太陽橫過西方的海面時，對著東方留下它的最後
的敬禮。

The sun goes to cross the Western sea, leaving its last
salutation to the East.

43 /

枯竭的河床，並不感謝它的過去。

The dry river-bed finds no thanks for its past.

44 /

你看不見你自己，你所看見的只是你的影子。

What you are you do not see, what you see is your shadow.

45 /

神自己的清晨，在祂自己看來也是新奇的。

His own mornings are new surprises to God.

46 /

不要因為你自己沒有胃口，而去責備你的食物。

Do not blame your food because you have no appetite.

47 /

群樹如表示大地的願望似的，踮起腳來向天空窺望。

The trees, like the longings of the earth, stand a-tiptoe to peep at the heaven.

48 /

你微微笑著，不同我說什麼話。而我覺得，為此，我已等待很久了。

You smiled and talked to me of nothing and I felt that for this I had been waiting long.

29

49 /

謝謝神，我不是一個權力的輪子，而是被壓在這輪子下的活人之一。

I thank thee that I am none of the wheels of power but I am one with the living creatures that are crushed by it.

50 /

你的偶像委散在塵土中了，這可證明神的塵土比你的偶像還偉大。

Your idol is shattered in the dust to prove that God's dust is greater than your idol.

51 /

絕不要害怕剎那——永恆之聲這樣唱著。

Never be afraid of the moments — thus sings the voice of the everlasting.

52 /

當我們是大為謙卑的時候，便是我們最近於偉大的
時候。

We come nearest to the great when we are great in humility.

53 /

神從創造中找到祂自己。

God finds himself by creating.

54 /

人在他的歷史中表現不出自己，他在歷史中奮鬥著
露出頭角。

Man does not reveal himself in his history, he struggles up
through it.

55 /

水裡的游魚是沉默的，陸地上的獸類是喧鬧的，空中的飛鳥是歌唱著的。

但是，人類卻兼有海裡的沉默、地上的喧鬧與空中的音樂。

The fish in the water is silent, the animal on the earth is noisy, the bird in the air is singing.

But Man has in him the silence of the sea, the noise of the earth and the music of the air.

56 /

心是尖銳的，不是寬博的，它執著在每一點上，卻並不活動。

The mind, sharp but not broad, sticks at every point but does not move.

57 /

我的白晝已經完了，我像一隻泊在海灘上的小船，諦聽著晚潮跳舞的樂聲。

My day is done, and I am like a boat drawn on the beach, listening to the dance-music of the tide in the evening.

58 /

在我自己的杯中，飲了我的酒吧，朋友。
一倒在別人的杯裡，這酒騰跳的泡沫便要消失了。
Take my wine in my own cup, friend.
It loses its wreath of foam when poured into that of others.

59 /

我們的生命是天賦的，我們唯有獻出生命，才能得
到生命。
Life is given to us, we earn it by giving it.

60 /

麻雀看見孔雀負擔著它的翎尾，替它擔憂。
The sparrow is sorry for the peacock at the burden of its tail.

61　/

颱風於無路之中尋求最短之路，又突然地在「無何有之國」終止它的尋求了。

The hurricane seeks the shortest road by the no-road, and suddenly ends its search in the Nowhere.

62　/

瀑布歌唱道：「雖然口渴的人只要少許的水便夠了，我卻很快活地給了我全部的水。」

"I give my whole water in joy," sings the waterfall, "though little of it is enough for the thirsty."

63　/

神對人說：「我要醫治你，因此傷害你；要愛你，因此懲罰你。」

God says to man, "I heal you therefore I hurt, love you therefore punish."

64 /

神對於那些大帝國會感到厭惡，卻絕不會厭惡那些
小小的花朵。

God grows weary of great kingdoms, but never of little
flowers.

65 /

把那些花朵拋擲上去的無休無止的狂歡大喜，其源
泉是在哪裡呢？

Where is the fountain that throws up these flowers in a
ceaseless outbreak of ecstasy?

66 /

幼花的蓓蕾開放了，它叫道：「親愛的世界呀，請
不要萎謝了。」

The infant flower opens its bud and cries, "Dear World,
please do not fade."

67 /

詩人的風,正出經海洋和森林,追求它自己的歌聲。

The poet wind is out over the sea and the forest to seek his own voice.

68 /

這寡獨的黃昏,幕著霧與雨,我在我的心的孤寂裡,感覺到它的歎息。

In my solitude of heart I feel the sigh of this widowed evening veiled with mist and rain.

69 /

錯誤禁不起失敗,但是真理卻不怕失敗。

Wrong cannot afford defeat but Right can.

70 /

霧，像愛情一樣，在山峰的心上遊戲，生出種種美麗的變幻。

The mist, like love, plays upon the heart of the hills and brings out surprises of beauty.

71 /

謝謝火焰給你光明，但是不要忘了那執燈的人，他是堅忍地站在黑暗當中呢。

Thank the flame for its light, but do not forget the lampholder standing in the shade with constancy of patience.

72 /

樵夫的斧頭，問樹要斧柄。
樹便給了他。

The woodcutter's axe begged for its handle from the tree.
The tree gave it.

37

73 /

我的朋友，你的語聲飄蕩在我的心裡，像那海水的
低吟聲繚繞在靜聽著的松林之間。

Your voice, my friend, wanders in my heart, like the muffled
sound of the sea among these listening pines.

74 /

小草呀，你的足步雖小，但是你擁有你足下的土地。

Tiny grass, your steps are small, but you possess the earth
under your tread.

75 /

貞操是從豐富的愛情中生出來的財富。

Chastity is a wealth that comes from abundance of love.

76 /

我們把世界看錯了，反說它欺騙我們。

We read the world wrong and say that it deceives us.

77 /

「完全」為了對「不全」的愛，把自己裝飾得美麗。

The Perfect decks itself in beauty for the love of the Imperfect.

78 /

綠草求她地上的伴侶。
樹木求他天空的寂寞。

The grass seeks her crowd in the earth.
The tree seeks his solitude of the sky.

79 /

在死的時候，眾多合而為一；在生的時候，一化為眾多。

神死了的時候，宗教便將合而為一。

In death the many becomes one; in life the one becomes many.

Religion will be one when God is dead.

80 /

每一個孩子出生時都帶來訊息說：神對人並未灰心失望。

Every child comes with the message that God is not yet discouraged of man.

81 /

那想做好人的，在門外敲著門；那愛人的，看見門敞開著。

He who wants to do good knocks at the gate; he who loves finds the gate open.

82 /

露珠對湖水說道：「你是在荷葉下面的大露珠，我是在荷葉上面的較小的露珠。」

"You are the big drop of dew under the lotus leaf, I am the smaller one on its upper side," said the dewdrop to the lake.

83 /

藝術家是自然的情人，所以他是自然的奴隸，也是自然的主人。

The artist is the lover of Nature, therefore he is her slave and her master.

84 /

使生如夏花之絢爛，死如秋葉之靜美。

Let life be beautiful like summer flowers and death like autumn leaves.

41

85 /

人對他自己建築起堤防來。

Man barricades against himself.

86 /

這個不可見的黑暗之火焰，以繁星為其火花的，到底是什麼呢？

What is this unseen flame of darkness whose sparks are the stars?

87 /

「你離我有多遠呢，果實呀？」
「我藏在你心裡呢，花呀。」

"How far are you from me, O Fruit?"
"I am hidden in your heart, O Flower."

88 /

這個渴望是為了那個在黑夜裡感覺得到，在大白天裡卻看不見的人。

This longing is for the one who is felt in the dark, but not seen in the day.

89 /

綠葉的生與死乃是旋風的急驟旋轉，它的更廣大的旋轉圈子乃是在天上繁星之間徐緩地轉動。

The birth and death of the leaves are the rapid whirls of the eddy whose wider circles move slowly among stars.

90 /

在黑暗中，「一」視若一體；在光亮中，「一」便視若眾多。

In darkness the One appears as uniform; in the light the One appears as manifold.

91 /

刀鞘保護刀的鋒利，它自己則滿足於它的遲鈍。

The scabbard is content to be dull when it protects the keenness of the sword.

92 /

大地借助於綠草，顯出她自己的殷勤好客。

The great earth makes herself hospitable with the help of the grass.

93 /

我靈魂裡的憂鬱就是她的新婚面紗。
這面紗等候著在夜間卸去。

The sadness of my soul is her bride's veil.
It waits to be lifted in the night.

94 /

安靜些吧，我的心，這些大樹都是祈禱者呀。

Be still, my heart, these great trees are prayers.

95 /

死之印記給生的錢幣以價值，使它能夠用生命來購買那真正的寶物。

Death's stamp gives value to the coin of life; making it possible to buy with life what is truly precious.

96 /

白雲謙遜地站在天之一隅。
晨光給它戴上霞彩。

The cloud stood humbly in a corner of the sky.
The morning crowned it with splendor.

97 /

濃霧彷彿是大地的願望。
它藏起了太陽，而太陽原是她所呼求的。

The mist is like the earth's desire.
It hides the sun for whom she cries.

98 /

我想起了浮泛在生與愛與死的川流上的許多別的時
代，以及這些時代之被遺忘，我便感覺到離開塵世
的自由了。

I think of other ages that floated upon the stream of life and
love and death and are forgotten, and I feel the freedom of
passing away.

99 /

根是地下的枝。
枝是空中的根。

Roots are the branches down in the earth.
Branches are roots in the air.

100 /

瞬刻的喧聲，譏笑著永恆的音樂。

The noise of the moment scoffs at the music of the Eternal.

101 /

只管走過去，不必逗留著採了花朵來保存，因為一路上花朵自會繼續綻放。

Do not linger to gather flowers to keep them, but walk on, for flowers will keep themselves blooming all your way.

102 /

遠遠去了的夏之音樂，翱翔於秋間，尋求它的舊壘。

The music of the far-away summer flutters around the autumn seeking its former nest.

103 /

塵土受到損辱，卻以她的花朵來報答。

The dust receives insult and in return offers her flowers.

104 /

不要從你自己的袋裡掏出勳績借給你的朋友，這是汙辱他的。

Do not insult your friend by lending him merits from your own pocket.

105 /

無名的日子的感觸，攀緣在我的心上，正像那綠色的苔蘚，攀緣在老樹的周身。

The touch of the nameless days clings to my heart like mosses round the old tree.

106 /

權勢對世界說道：「你是我的。」
世界便把權勢囚禁在她的寶座下面。
愛情對世界說道：「我是你的。」
世界便給予愛情以在她屋內來往的自由。

Power said to the world, "You are mine."
The world kept it prisoner on her throne.
Love said to the world, "I am thine."
The world gave it the freedom of her house.

107 /

回聲嘲笑著她的原聲，以證明她是原聲。

The echo mocks her origin to prove she is the original.

108 /

當富貴利達的人誇說他得到神的特別恩惠時，神卻
羞愧了。

God is ashamed when the prosperous boasts of his special favour.

109 /

我投射我自己的影子在我的路上，因為我有一盞還沒有燃點起來的明燈。

I cast my own shadow upon my path, because I have a lamp that has not been lighted.

110 /

人走進喧嘩的群眾裡去，為的是要淹沒他自己的沉默的呼號。

Man goes into the noisy crowd to drown his own clamour of silence.

111 /

太陽只穿一件樸素的光衣，白雲卻披了燦爛的裙裾。

The sun has his simple robe of light. The clouds are decked with gorgeousness.

112 /

終止於衰竭的是「死亡」，但「圓滿」卻終止於無窮。

That which ends in exhaustion is death, but the perfect ending is in the endless.

113 /

今天大地在太陽光裡向我營營哼鳴，像一個織著布的婦人，用一種已經被忘卻的語言，哼著一些古代的歌曲。

The earth hums to me today in the sun, like a woman at her spinning, some ballad of the ancient time in a forgotten tongue.

114 /

綠草是無愧於它所生長的偉大世界的。

The grass-blade is worthy of the great world where it grows.

51

115 /

權勢以它的惡行自誇，落下的黃葉與浮游的雲片卻
在笑它。

The power that boasts of its mischiefs is laughed at by the
yellow leaves that fall, and clouds that pass by.

116 /

山峰如群兒之喧嚷，舉起他們的雙臂，想去捉天上
的星星。

The hills are like shouts of children who raise their arms,
trying to catch stars.

117 /

道路雖然擁擠，卻是寂寞的，因為它是不被愛的。

The road is lonely in its crowd for it is not loved.

118 /

夢是一個一定要談話的妻子。
睡眠是一個默默忍受的丈夫。

Dream is a wife who must talk.
Sleep is a husband who silently suffers.

119 /

夜與逝去的日子接吻，輕輕地在他耳旁說道：「我
是死，是你的母親。我就要給你以新的生命。」

The night kisses the fading day whispering to his ear, "I am
death, your mother. I am to give you fresh birth."

120 /

黑夜呀，我感覺到你的美了。你的美如一個可愛的
女人，當她把燈滅了的時候。

I feel thy beauty, dark night, like that of the loved woman
when she has put out the lamp.

121 /

我把在那些已逝去的世界上的繁榮帶到我的世界上來。

I carry in my world that flourishes the worlds that have failed.

122 /

鳥以為把魚舉在空中是一種慈善的舉動。

The bird thinks it is an act of kindness to give the fish a life in the air.

123 /

親愛的朋友呀，當我靜聽著海濤時，我好幾次在暮色深沉的黃昏裡，在這個海岸上，感到你的偉大思想的沉默了。

Dear friend, I feel the silence of your great thoughts of many a deepening eventide on this beach when I listen to these waves.

124 /

夜對太陽說道：「在月亮中，你送了你的情書給我。」

「我已在綠草上留下我流著淚點的回答了。」

"In the moon thou sendest thy love letters to me," said the night to the sun.

"I leave my answers in tears upon the grass."

125 /

偉人是一個天生的孩子，當他死時，他把他偉大的孩提時代給了世界。

The great is a born child; when he dies he gives his great childhood to the world.

126 /

不是槌的打擊，乃是水的載歌載舞，使鵝卵石臻於完美。

Not hammer-strokes, but dance of the water sings the pebbles into perfection.

127 /

蜜蜂從花中啜蜜，離開時嚶嚶地道謝。

浮華的蝴蝶卻相信花是應該向它道謝的。

Bees sip honey from flowers and hum their thanks when they leave.

The gaudy butterfly is sure that the flowers owe thanks to him.

128 /

如果你不等待著要說出完全的真理，那麼把真話說出來是很容易的。

To be outspoken is easy when you do not wait to speak the complete truth.

129 /

「可能」問「不可能」道：「你住在什麼地方呢？」

它回答道：「在那無能為力者的夢境裡。」

Asks the Possible to the Impossible,

  "Where is your dwelling-place?"

  "In the dreams of the impotent," comes the answer.

130 /

如果你把所有的錯誤都關在門外時，真理也要被關
在門外面了。

If you shut your door to all errors truth will be shut out.

131 /

我聽見有些東西在我心的憂悶後面蕭蕭作響，——
我不能看見它們。

I hear some rustle of things behind my sadness of heart, — I
cannot see them.

132 /

閒暇在動作時便是工作。
靜止的海水蕩動時便成波濤。

Leisure in its activity is work.
The stillness of the sea stirs in waves.

133　/

綠葉戀愛時便成了花。
花崇拜時便成了果實。

The leaf becomes flower when it loves.
The flower becomes fruit when it worships.

134　/

埋在地下的樹根使樹枝產生果實，卻不要什麼報酬。

The roots below the earth claim no rewards for making the
branches fruitful.

135　/

陰雨的黃昏，風無休止地吹著。
我看著搖曳的樹枝，想念著萬物的偉大。

This rainy evening the wind is restless.
I look at the swaying branches and ponder over the greatness
of all things.

136 /

讓我設想，在群星之中，有一顆星是指導著我的生命通過不可知的黑暗的。

Let me think that there is one among those stars that guides my life through the dark unknown.

137 /

女人，你用了你美麗的手指，觸著我的什物，秩序便如音樂似的生出來了。

Woman, with the grace of your fingers you touched my things and order came out like music.

138 /

子夜的風雨，如一個巨大的孩子，在不合時宜的黑夜裡醒來，開始遊戲和喧鬧。

Storm of midnight, like a giant child awakened in the untimely dark, has begun to play and shout.

139 /

海呀，你這暴風雨的孤寂的新嫁娘呀，你雖掀起波浪追隨你的情人，但是無用呀。

Thou raisest thy waves vainly to follow thy lover, O sea, thou lonely bride of the storm.

140 /

文字對工作說道：「我慚愧我的空虛。」

工作對文字說道：「當我看見你時，我便知道我是怎樣的貧乏了。」

"I am ashamed of my emptiness, " said the Word to the Work.

"I know how poor I am when I see you, " said the Work to the Word.

141 /

時間是變化的財富。時鐘模仿它，卻只有變化而無財富。

Time is the wealth of change, but the clock in its parody makes it mere change and no wealth.

142 /

真理穿了衣裳，覺得事實太拘束了。
在想像中，她卻轉動得很舒暢。

Truth in her dress finds facts too tight.
In fiction she moves with ease.

143 /

當我到這裡那裡旅行著時，路呀，我厭倦你了；
但是現在，當你引導我到各處去時，我便愛上你，
與你結婚了。

When I travelled to here and to there, I was tired of thee, O
Road,
but now when thou leadest me to everywhere I am wedded
to thee in love.

144 /

一個憂鬱的聲音，築巢於逝水似的年華中。
它在夜裡向我唱道：「我愛你。」

One sad voice has its nest among the ruins of the years.
It sings to me in the night, — "I loved you."

145 /

燃著的火，以它熊熊的光焰警告我不要走近它。
把我從潛藏在灰中的餘燼裡救出來吧。

The flaming fire warns me off by its own glow.
Save me from the dying embers hidden under ashes.

146 /

在黃昏的微光裡，有那清晨的鳥兒來到了我沉默的
鳥巢裡。

In the dusk of the evening the bird of some early dawn comes
to the nest of my silence.

147 /

生命裡留了許多罅隙，從中送來了死之憂鬱的音樂。

Gaps are left in life through which comes the sad music of
death.

148 /

神的巨大的威權是在柔和的微颸裡，而不在狂風暴
雨之中。

God's great power is in the gentle breeze, not in the storm.

149 /

我有群星在天上。
但是，唉，我屋裡的小燈卻沒有點亮。

I have my stars in the sky.
But oh for my little lamp unlit in my house.

150 /

死文字的塵土沾著你。
用沉默去洗淨你的靈魂吧。

The dust of the dead words clings to thee.
Wash thy soul with silence.

151　/

在夢中，一切事都散漫著，都壓著我，但這不過是一個夢呀。

當我醒來時，我便將覺得這些事都已聚集在你那裡，我也便將自由了。

This is a dream in which things are all loose and they oppress. I shall find them gathered in thee when I awake and shall be free.

152　/

我的思想隨著這些閃耀的綠葉而閃耀；我的心靈因了這日光的撫觸而歌唱；我的生命因為偕了萬物一同浮泛在空間的蔚藍、時間的墨黑中而感到歡快。

My thoughts shimmer with these shimmering leaves and my heart sings with the touch of this sunlight; my life is glad to be floating with all things into the blue of space, into the dark of time.

153 /

當人微笑時，世界愛了他；但他大笑時，世界便怕
他了。

The world loved man when he smiled. The world became
afraid of him when he laughed.

154 /

沉默蘊蓄著語聲，正如鳥巢擁圍著睡鳥。

Silence will carry your voice like the nest that holds the
sleeping birds.

155 /

落日問道：「有誰繼續我的職務呢？」
瓦燈說道：「我要盡我所能地做去，我的主人。」

"Who is there to take up my duties?" asked the setting sun.
"I shall do what I can, my Master," said the earthen lamp.

156 /

採著花瓣時，得不到花的美麗。

By plucking her petals you do not gather the beauty of the
flower.

157 /

夜祕密地把花開放了，卻讓白日去領受謝詞。

The night opens the flowers in secret and allows the day to get thanks.

158 /

世界已在早晨敞開了它的光明之心。
出來吧，我的心，帶著你的愛去與它相會。

The world has opened its heart of light in the morning.
Come out, my heart, with thy love to meet it.

159 /

大的不怕與小的同遊。
居中的卻遠而避之。

The Great walks with the Small without fear.
The Middling keeps aloof.

160 /

權勢認為犧牲者的痛苦是忘恩負義。

Power takes as ingratitude the writhings of its victims.

161 /

思想掠過我的心上，如一群野鴨飛過天空。
我聽見它們的鼓翼之聲了。

Thoughts pass in my mind like flocks of ducks in the sky.
I hear the voice of their wings.

162 /

當我們以我們的充實為樂時，那麼，我們便能很快
樂地跟我們的果實分手了。

When we rejoice in our fulness, then we can part with our
fruits with joy.

163 /

雨點吻著大地，微語道：「母親，我們是你思家的孩子，現在從天上回到你這裡來了。」

The raindrops kissed the earth and whispered, — "We are thy homesick children, mother, come back to thee from the heaven."

164 /

蛛網像是要捉露點，卻捉住了蒼蠅。

The cobweb pretends to catch dewdrops and catches flies.

165 /

世界以它的痛苦同我接吻，而要求歌聲做報酬。

The world has kissed my soul with its pain, asking for its return in songs.

166 /

螢火蟲對天上的星說道：「學者說你的光明總有一天
會消滅的。」
天上的星不回答它。

"The learned say that your lights will one day be no more,"
said the firefly to the stars.
The stars made no answer.

167 /

思想以它自己的語言餵養它自己而成長起來了。
Thought feeds itself with its own words and grows.

168 /

溝洫總喜歡想：河流的存在，是專為它供給水流的。
The canal loves to think that rivers exist solely to supply it with
water.

175　/

雲把水倒在河的水杯裡，它們自己卻藏在遠山之中。

The clouds fill the water-cups of the river, hiding themselves in the distant hills.

176　/

我一路走去，從我的水瓶中漏出水來。
只剩下極少極少的水供我回家使用了。

I spill water from my waterjar as I walk on my way,
Very little remains for my home.

177　/

杯中的水是光輝的；海中的水卻是黑色的。
小理可以用文字來說清楚；大理卻只有沉默。

The water in a vessel is sparkling; the water in the sea is dark.
The small truth has words that are clear; the great truth has great silence.

178 /

女人呀，你用眼淚的深邃包繞著世界的心，正如大
海包繞著大地。

Woman, thou hast encircled the world's heart with the depth
of thy tears as the sea has the earth.

179 /

我像那夜間之路，正靜悄悄地諦聽著記憶的足音。

I am like the road in the night listening to the footfalls of its
memories in silence.

180 /

你的微笑是你自己田園裡的花，你的談吐是你自己
山上的松林的蕭蕭；但是你的心呀，卻是那個女人，
那個我們全都認識的女人。

Your smile was the flowers of your own fields, your talk was
the rustle of your own mountain pines, but your heart was
the woman that we all know.

181 /

黃昏的天空，在我看來，像一扇窗戶，一盞燈火，
燈火背後的一次等待。

The evening sky to me is like a window, and a lighted lamp,
and a waiting behind it.

182 /

太陽以微笑向我問候。
雨，他的憂悶的姊姊，向我的心談話。

The sunshine greets me with a smile.
The rain, his sad sister, talks to my heart.

183 /

太急於做好事的人，反而找不到時間去做好人。

He who is too busy doing good finds no time to be good.

184　/

我把小小的禮物留給我所愛的人，—— 大的禮物卻
留給一切的人。

It is the little things that I leave behind for my loved ones, —
great things are for everyone.

185　/

黑暗向光明旅行，但是盲者卻向死亡旅行。

Darkness travels towards light, but blindness towards death.

186　/

我是秋雲，空空地不載著雨水，但在成熟的稻田
中，看見了我的充實。

I am the autumn cloud, empty of rain, see my fulness in the
field of ripened rice.

187　/

我的晝間之花，落下它那被遺忘的花瓣。
在黃昏中，這花成熟為一顆記憶的金果。

My flower of the day dropped its petals forgotten.
In the evening it ripens into a golden fruit of memory.

188　/

蟋蟀的唧唧，夜雨的淅瀝，從黑暗中傳到我的耳
邊，好似我已逝的少年時代沙沙地來到我夢境中。

The cricket's chirp and the patter of rain come to me through
the dark, like the rustle of dreams from my past youth.

189　/

靜靜地坐著吧，我的心，不要揚起你的塵土。
讓世界自己尋路向你走來。

Sit still, my heart, do not raise your dust.
Let the world find its way to you.

76

190 /

這世界乃是為美之音樂所馴服了的狂風驟雨的世界。

This world is the world of wild storms kept tame with the music of beauty.

191 /

他們嫉妒，他們殘殺，世人反而稱讚他們。

然而神卻害了羞，匆匆地把祂的記憶埋藏在綠草下面。

They hated and killed and men praised them.
But God in shame hastens to hide its memory under the green grass.

192 /

女人，在你的笑聲裡有著生命之泉的音樂。

Woman, in your laughter you have the music of the fountain of life.

77

193 /

弓在箭要射出之前，低聲對箭說道：「你的自由就是我的自由。」

The bow whispers to the arrow before it speeds forth — "Your freedom is mine."

194 /

腳趾乃是捨棄了其過去的手指。

Toes are the fingers that have forsaken their past.

195 /

神愛人間的燈光甚於他自己的大星。

God loves man's lamp-lights better than his own great stars.

196 /

全是理智的心，恰如一柄全是鋒刃的刀。
它叫使用它的人手上流血。

A mind all logic is like a knife all blade.
It makes the hand bleed that uses it.

197 /

花朵向星辰落盡了的曙天叫道：「我的露點全失落
了。」

"I have lost my dewdrop," cried the flower to the morning
sky that has lost all its stars.

198 /

晚霞向太陽說道：「我的心經了你的接吻，便似金
的寶箱了。」

"My heart is like the golden casket of thy kiss," said the
sunset cloud to the sun.

199 /

燃燒著的木塊，熊熊地生出火光，叫道：「這是我的花朵，我的死亡。」

The burning log bursts in flame and cries, — "This is my flower, my death."

200 /

小狗疑心大宇宙陰謀篡奪它的位置。

The pet dog suspects the universe for scheming to take its place.

201 /

河岸向河流說道：「我不能留住你的波浪。
讓我保存你的足印在我的心裡吧。」

"I cannot keep your waves," says the bank to the river.
"Let me keep your footprints in my heart."

202 /

接觸著，你也許會殺害；遠離著，你也許會占有。

By touching you may kill, by keeping away you may possess.

203 /

黃蜂認為鄰蜂儲蜜之巢太小。
他的鄰人要他去建一個更小的。

The wasp thinks that the honeyhive of the neighbouring bees
is too small.
His neighbours ask him to build one still smaller.

204 /

白日以這小小地球的喧擾，淹沒了整個宇宙的沉默。

The day, with the noise of this little earth, drowns the silence
of all worlds.

205 /

太陽在西方落下時，他的早晨的東方已靜悄悄地站在他面前。

When the sun goes down to the West, the East of his morning stands before him in silence.

206 /

我的晚色從陌生的樹木中走來，它用我的曉星所不懂得的語言說話。

My evening came among the alien trees and spoke in a language which my morning stars did not know.

207 /

讓我不要錯誤地把自己放在我的世界裡而使它反對我。

Let me not put myself wrongly to my world and set it against me.

208 /

榮譽使我感到慚愧，因為我暗地裡求著它。

Praise shames me, for I secretly beg for it.

209 /

愛就是充實了的生命，正如盛滿了酒的酒杯。

Love is life in its fulness like the cup with its wine.

210 /

當我沒有什麼事做時，便讓我不做什麼事，不受騷擾地沉入安靜深處吧，一如那海水沉默時海邊的暮色。

Let my doing nothing when I have nothing to do become untroubled in its depth of peace like the evening in the seashore when the water is silent.

211 /

少女呀，你的純樸，如湖水之碧，表現出你的真理之深邃。

Maiden, your simplicity, like the blueness of the lake, reveals your depth of truth.

212 /

最好的東西不是獨來的，
它伴了所有的東西同來。

The best does not come alone.
It comes with the company of the all.

213 /

歌聲在空中感到無限，圖畫在地上感到無限，詩呢，無論在空中、在地上都是如此。
因為詩的詞句含有能走動的意義與能飛翔的音樂。

The song feels the infinite in the air, the picture in the earth, the poem in the air and the earth;
For its words have meaning that walks and music that soars.

214 /

我們的欲望把彩虹的顏色借給那只不過是雲霧的人生。

Our desire lends the colours of the rainbow to the mere mists and vapours of life.

215 /

我的心向著闌珊的風張了帆,要到無論何處的蔭涼之島去。

My heart has spread its sails to the idle winds for the shadowy island of Anywhere.

216 /

神等待著,要從人的手上把祂自己的花朵作為禮物贏回去。

God waits to win back his own flowers as gifts from man's hands.

85

217 /

我的憂思纏擾著我，要問我它們自己的名字。

My sad thoughts tease me asking me their own names.

218 /

在這喧嘩的波濤起伏的海中，我渴望著詠歌之島。

I long for the Island of Songs across this heaving Sea of Shouts.

219 /

死之流泉，使生的止水跳躍。

The fountain of death makes the still water of life play.

220 /

果實的事業是尊貴的，花的事業是甜美的，但是讓
我做葉的事業吧，葉是謙遜地、專心地垂著綠蔭
的。

The service of the fruit is precious, the service of the flower
is sweet, but let my service be the service of the leaves in its
shade of humble devotion.

221 /

我的朋友，你偉大的心閃射出東方朝陽的光芒，正
如黎明中的一個積雪的孤峰。

My friend, your great heart shone with the sunrise of the East
like the snowy summit of a lonely hill in the dawn.

222 /

那些有一切東西而沒有您的人，我的神，在譏笑著
那些沒別的東西而只有您的人呢。

Those who have everything but thee, my God, laugh at those
who have nothing but thyself.

223 /

把我當作你的杯吧，讓我為了你，為了你的人而盛滿了水吧。

Make me thy cup and let my fulness be for thee and for thine.

224 /

狂風暴雨像是在痛苦中的某個天神的哭聲，因為他的愛情被大地所拒絕。

The storm is like the cry of some god in pain whose love the earth refuses.

225 /

世界不會流失，因為死亡並不是一個罅隙。

The world does not leak because death is not a crack.

226 /

夜之黑暗是一隻口袋，迸出黎明的金光。

Night's darkness is a bag that bursts with the gold of the dawn.

227 /

讓睜眼看著玫瑰花的人也看看它的刺。

Let him only see the thorns who has eyes to see the rose.

228 /

群眾是凶暴的，但個人是善良的。

Men are cruel, but Man is kind.

89

229 /

生命因為付出了的愛情而更為富足。

Life has become richer by the love that has been lost.

230 /

踢足只能從地上揚起塵土而不能得到收穫。

Kicks only raise dust and not crops from the earth.

231 /

爆竹呀，你對群星的侮蔑，又跟著你自己回到地上來了。

Rockets, your insult to the stars follows yourself back to the earth.

232 /

不要說「這是早晨」，別用一個「昨天」的名詞把它打發掉。

把它當作第一次看到的還沒有名字的新生孩子吧。

Do not say, "It is morning," and dismiss it with a name of yesterday.

See it for the first time as a new-born child that has no name.

233 /

我們的名字，便是夜裡海波上發出的光，痕跡也不留地就泯滅了。

Our names are the light that glows on the sea waves at night and then dies without leaving its signature.

234 /

雨點向茉莉花微語道：「把我永久地留在你的心裡吧。」

茉莉花歎息了一聲，落在地上了。

The raindrop whispered to the jasmine, "Keep me in your heart for ever." The jasmine sighed, "Alas," and dropped to the ground.

235 /

生命的運動在它自己的音樂裡得以休息。

The movement of life has its rest in its own music.

236 /

鳥翼上繫了黃金，這鳥便永不能再在天上翱翔了。

Set the bird's wings with gold and it will never again soar in the sky.

237 /

在心的遠景裡，那相隔的距離顯得更廣闊了。

In heart's perspective the distance looms large.

238 /

真理之川從它的錯誤之溝渠中流過。

The stream of truth flows through its channels of mistakes.

239 /

我們那一帶的荷花又在這陌生的水上開了花，放出
同樣的清香，只是名字換了。

The same lotus of our clime blooms here in the alien water
with the same sweetness, under another name.

240 /

青煙對天空誇口，灰燼對大地誇口，都以為它們是
火的兄弟。

Smoke boasts to the sky, and Ashes to the earth, that they are
brothers to the fire.

241　/

今天我的心是在想家了，在想著那跨過時間之海的
那一個甜蜜的時候。

My heart is homesick today for the one sweet hour across the
sea of time.

242　/

膽怯的思想呀，不要怕我。
我是一個詩人。

Timid thoughts, do not be afraid of me.
I am a poet.

243　/

我們的生命就似渡過一個大海，我們都相聚在這個
狹小的舟中。
死時，我們便到了岸，各往各的世界去了。

This life is the crossing of a sea, where we meet in the same
narrow ship.
In death we reach the shore and go to our different worlds.

244 /

月兒把她的光明遍照在天上，卻留著黑斑給她自己。

The moon has her light all over the sky, her dark spots to herself.

245 /

您曾經帶領著我，穿過我白天擁擠不堪的旅程，而到達我黃昏的孤寂之境。

在通宵的寂靜裡，我等待著它的意義。

Thou hast led me through my crowded travels of the day to my evening's loneliness.

I wait for its meaning through the stillness of the night.

246 /

我的心在朦朧的沉默裡，似乎充滿了蟋蟀的鳴聲——那灰色而微明的歌聲。

The dim silence of my mind seems filled with crickets' chirp — the grey twilight of sound.

247 /

晨光問毛茛道：「你是驕傲得不肯和我接吻麼？」

"Are you too proud to kiss me?" the morning light asked
the buttercup.

248 /

小花問道：「我要怎樣地對你唱，怎樣地崇拜你呢，
太陽呀？」
太陽答道：「只要用你純潔而素樸的沉默。」

"How may I sing to thee and worship, O Sun?" asked the
little flower.

"By the simple silence of thy purity," answered the sun.

249 /

夜的沉默，如一個深深的燈盞，銀河便是它燃著的
燈光。

The night's silence, like a deep lamp, is burning with the light
of its milky way.

250 /

死像大海的無限歌聲，日夜衝擊著生命的光明島的
四周。

Around the sunny island of Life swells day and night death's
limitless song of the sea.

251 /

黑雲受光的親吻時便變成天上的花朵。

Dark clouds become heaven's flowers when kissed by light.

252 /

不要讓刀鋒譏笑它柄子的拙鈍。

Let not the sword-blade mock its handle for being blunt.

97

253 /

人是獸時，他比獸還壞。

Man is worse than an animal when he is an animal.

254 /

鳥的歌聲是曙光從大地反響過去的回聲。

The bird-song is the echo of the morning light back from the earth.

255 /

花瓣似的山峰在飲著日光，這山豈不像一朵花嗎？

Is not this mountain like a flower, with its petals of hill, drinking the sunlight?

256 /

「真實」的含義被誤解，輕重被倒置，那就成了「不真實」。

The real with its meaning read wrong and emphasis misplaced is the unreal.

257 /

道旁的草，愛那天上的星吧，你的夢境便可在花朵裡實現了。

Wayside grass, love the star, then your dreams will come out in flowers.

258 /

這樹的顫動之葉，觸動著我的心，像嬰兒的手指。

The trembling leaves of this tree touch my heart like the fingers of an infant child.

259　/

我的心呀，從世界的流動中找你的美吧，正如那小船得到風與水的優美似的。

Find your beauty, my heart, from the world's movement, like the boat that has the grace of the wind and the water.

260　/

虛偽永遠不能憑藉它生長在權力中而變成真實。

The false can never grow into truth by growing in power.

261　/

我的心，同著它的歌的拍拍舐岸的波浪，渴望著要撫愛這個陽光熙和的綠色世界。

My heart, with its lapping waves of song, longs to caress this green world of the sunny day.

262 /

我住在我的這個小小的世界裡，生怕使它再縮小一丁點兒。把我抬舉到您的世界裡去吧，讓我高高興興地失去我的一切自由。

I live in this little world of mine and am afraid to make it the least less. Lift me into thy world and let me have the freedom gladly to lose my all.

263 /

讓你的音樂如一柄利刃，直刺入市井喧擾的心中吧。

Let your music, like a sword, pierce the noise of the market to its heart.

264 /

小花睡在塵土裡。
它尋求蛺蝶走的道路。

The little flower lies in the dust.
It sought the path of the butterfly.

265 /

我是在道路縱橫的世界上。

夜來了。打開您的門吧，家之世界呵！

I am in the world of the roads.

The night comes. Open thy gate, thou world of the home.

266 /

我已經唱過了您白天的歌。

黃昏的時候，讓我拿著您的燈走過風雨飄搖的道路
吧。

I have sung the songs of thy day.

In the evening let me carry thy lamp through the stormy
path.

267 /

我不要求你進我的屋裡。

你到我無量的孤寂裡來吧，我的愛人！

I do not ask thee into the house.

Come into my infinite loneliness, my Lover.

268 /

死亡隸屬於生命，正與生一樣。

舉足是走路，正如落足也是走路。

Death belongs to life as birth does.

The walk is in the raising of the foot as in the laying of it down.

269 /

眼不能以視來驕人，卻以它們的眼鏡來驕人。

The eyes are not proud of their sight but of their eyeglasses.

270 /

我已經學會了你在花與陽光裡微語的意義。—— 再教我明白你在苦與死中所說的話吧。

I have learnt the simple meaning of thy whispers in flowers and sunshine — teach me to know thy words in pain and death.

271　/

夜的花朵來晚了，當早晨吻著她時，她戰慄著，歎息了一聲，萎落在地上了。

The night's flower was late when the morning kissed her, she shivered and sighed and dropped to the ground.

272　/

從萬物的愁苦中，我聽見了「永恆母親」的呻吟。

Through the sadness of all things I hear the crooning of the Eternal Mother.

273　/

大地呀，我到你岸上時是陌生人，住在你屋內時是賓客，離開你的門時是朋友。

I came to your shore as a stranger, I lived in your house as a guest, I leave your door as a friend, my earth.

274 /

當我去時，讓我的思想到你那裡來，如那夕陽的餘光，映在沉默的星天的邊上。

Let my thoughts come to you, when I am gone, like the after glow of sunset at the margin of starry silence.

275 /

當我死時，世界呀，請在你的沉默中，替我留著「我已經愛過了」這句話吧。

One word keep for me in thy silence, O World, when I am dead, "I have loved."

276 /

我們熱愛世界時便生活在這世界上。

We live in this world when we love it.

277 /

讓死者有那不朽的名，但讓生者有那不朽的愛。

Let the dead have the immortality of fame, but the living the immortality of love.

278 /

我看見你，像那半醒的嬰孩在黎明的微光裡看見他的母親，於是微笑而又睡去了。

I have seen thee as the half-awakened child sees his mother in the dusk of the dawn and then smiles and sleeps again.

279 /

我將死了又死，以明白生是無窮無盡的。

I shall die again and again to know that life is inexhaustible.

280 /

神的右手是慈愛的，但他的左手卻是可怕的。

God's right hand is gentle, but terrible is his left hand.

281 /

在我的心頭燃點起那休憩的黃昏星吧，然後讓黑夜
向我微語著愛情。

Light in my heart the evening star of rest and then let the
night whisper to me of love.

282 /

我是一個在黑暗中的孩子。
我從夜的被單裡向您伸出我的雙手，母親。

I am a child in the dark.
I stretch my hands through the coverlet of night for thee,
Mother.

283 /

白天的工作完了。把我的臉掩藏在您的臂間吧，母
親。

讓我入夢吧。

The day of work is done. Hide my face in your arms, Mother.
Let me dream.

284 /

集會時的燈光，點了很久，會散時，燈便立刻滅了。

The lamp of meeting burns long; it goes out in a moment at
the parting.

285 /

他們點了他們自己的燈，在他們的寺院裡，吟唱他
們自己的話語。

但是鳥兒卻在你的晨光中，唱著你的名字，——因
為你的名字便是快樂。

They light their own lamps and sing their own words in their
temples.

But the birds sing thy name in thine own morning light, —
for thy name is joy.

286 /

領我到您沉寂的中心，使我的心充滿了歌吧。

Lead me in the centre of thy silence to fill my heart with songs.

287 /

昨夜的風雨給今日的早晨戴上了金色的和平。

The storm of the last night has crowned this morning with golden peace.

288 /

讓那些選擇了他們自己的焰火嘶嘶的世界的，就生活在那裡吧。

我的心渴望著您的繁星，我的神。

Let them live who choose in their own hissing world of fireworks.

My heart longs for thy stars, my God.

289 /

愛的痛苦環繞著我的一生，像洶湧的大海似的唱著；而愛的快樂卻像鳥兒在花林裡似的唱著。

Love's pain sang round my life like the unplumbed sea, and love's joy sang like birds in its flowering groves.

290 /

真理彷彿帶了它的結論而來，而那結論卻產生了它的第二個。

Truth seems to come with its final word; and the final word gives birth to its next.

291 /

靜悄悄的黑夜具有母親的美麗，而吵鬧的白天具有孩子的美麗。

The silent night has the beauty of the mother and the clamorous day of the child.

292 /

真理引起了反對它自己的狂風驟雨，那場風雨吹散
了真理散播的種子。

Truth raises against itself the storm that scatters its seeds
broadcast.

293 /

假如您願意，您就熄了燈吧。
我將明白您的黑暗，而且將喜愛它。

Put out the lamp when thou wishest.
I shall know thy darkness and shall love it.

294 /

從別的日子裡飄浮到我的生命裡的雲，不再落下雨
點或引起風暴了，卻只給予我的夕陽的天空以色
彩。

Clouds come floating into my life from other days no longer
to shed rain or usher storm but to give colour to my sunset
sky.

295 /

當我在那日子的終了，站在您的面前時，您將看見我的傷疤，而知道我有我的許多創傷，但也有我的醫治之法。

When I stand before thee at the day's end thou shalt see my scars and know that I had my wounds and also my healing.

296 /

您的名字的甜蜜充溢著我的心，而我忘掉了我自己的──就像您的早晨的太陽升起時，那大霧便消失了。

Sweetness of thy name fills my heart when I forget mine — like thy morning sun when the mist is melted.

297 /

總有一天，我要在別的世界的晨光裡對你唱道：「我以前在地球的光裡，在人的愛裡，已經見過你了。」

Some day I shall sing to thee in the sunrise of some other world, "I have seen thee before in the light of the earth, in the love of man."

298　/

雨中的溼土的氣息，就像從渺小的無聲群眾那裡來
的一陣巨大的讚美歌聲。

The smell of the wet earth in the rain rises like a great chant
of praise from the voiceless multitude of the insignificant.

299　/

您的陽光對著我心頭的冬天微笑著，從來不懷疑它
春天的花朵。

Thy sunshine smiles upon the winter days of my heart, never
doubting of its spring flowers.

300　/

這一天是不快活的。光在蹙額的雲下，如一個挨打
的兒童，灰白的臉上留著淚痕；風又號叫著，似一
個受傷的世界的哭聲。但是我知道，我正跋涉著去
會我的朋友。

Cheerless is the day, the light under frowning clouds is like
a punished child with traces of tears on its pale cheeks, and
the cry of the wind is like the cry of a wounded world. But I
know I am travelling to meet my Friend.

301 /

神等待著人在智慧中重新獲得童年。

God waits for man to regain his childhood in wisdom.

302 /

讓我感到這個世界乃是您的愛的成形吧，那麼，我的愛也將幫助著它。

Let me feel this world as thy love taking form, then my love will help it.

303 /

我夢見一顆星，一個光明島嶼，我將在那裡出生。在它快速的閒暇深處，我的生命將成熟它的事業，像秋天陽光下的稻田。

I dream of a star, an island of light, where I shall be born and in the depth of its quickening leisure my life will ripen its works like the rice-field in the autumn sun.

304 /

「永恆的旅客」呀，你可以在我的歌中找到你的足跡。

Thou wilt find, Eternal Traveller, marks of thy footsteps across my songs.

305 /

神在祂的愛裡吻著「有涯」，而人卻吻著「無涯」。

God kisses the finite in his love and man the infinite.

306 /

他是有福的，因為他的名望並沒有比他的真實更光亮。

Blessed is he whose fame does not outshine his truth.

307 /

神在我的黃昏的微光中，帶著花到我這裡來。這些花都是我過去之時的，在祂的花籃中還保存得很新鮮。

God comes to me in the dusk of my evening with the flowers from my past kept fresh in his basket.

308 /

夜的序曲是開始於夕陽西下的音樂，開始於它對難以形容的黑暗所作的莊嚴的讚歌。

The prelude of the night is commenced in the music of the sunset, in its solemn hymn to the ineffable dark.

309 /

有朝一日我們終會明白，死永遠不能夠奪去我們的靈魂所獲得的東西。因為她所獲得的，和她自己是一體。

We shall know some day that death can never rob us of that which our soul has gained, for her gains are one with herself.

310 /

當我和擁擠的人群一同在路上走過時，我看見您從
陽臺上送過來的微笑，我歌唱著，忘卻了所有的喧
嘩。

While I was passing with the crowd in the road I saw thy
smile from the balcony and I sang and forgot all noise.

311 /

讓我真真實實地活著吧，我的上帝。這樣，死對於
我也就成了真實的了。

Let me live truly, my Lord, so that death to me become true.

312 /

您越過不毛之年的沙漠而到達了圓滿的時刻。

Thou crossest desert lands of barren years to reach the
moment of fulfilment.

313 /

主呀，當我的生之琴弦都已調得諧和時，祢的手的一彈一奏，都可以發出愛的樂聲來。

When all the strings of my life will be tuned, my Master, then at every touch of thine will come out the music of love.

314 /

我的未完成的過去，從後面纏繞到我身上，使我難於死去。

請從它那裡釋放了我吧。

Release me from my unfulfilled past clinging to me from behind making death difficult.

315 /

這一刻我感到你的目光正落在我的心上，像那早晨陽光中的沉默落在已收穫的孤寂田野上一樣。

I feel thy gaze upon my heart this moment like the sunny silence of the morning upon the lonely field whose harvest is over.

316 /

我曾經受苦過，曾經失望過，曾經體會過「死亡」，
於是我以我在這偉大的世界裡為樂。

I have suffered and despaired and known death and I am glad
that I am in this great world.

317 /

讓我不至羞辱您吧，父親，您在您的孩子們身上顯
現出您的光榮。

Let me not shame thee, Father, who displayest thy glory in
thy children.

318 /

我攀登上高峰，發現在名譽的荒蕪不毛的高處，簡
直找不到遮身之地。我的引導者呵，領導著我在光
明逝去之前，進到沉靜的山谷裡去吧。在那裡，一
生的收穫將會成熟為黃金的智慧。

I have scaled the peak and found no shelter in fame's bleak
and barren height. Lead me, my Guide, before the light
fades, into the valley of quiet where life's harvest mellows
into golden wisdom.

319 /

人類的歷史默默忍耐地等待著受辱者的勝利。

Man's history is waiting in patience for the triumph of the insulted man.

320 /

在這個黃昏的朦朧裡，好些東西看來都彷彿如幻象一般——尖塔的底層在黑暗裡消失了，樹頂像是墨水模糊的斑點似的。我將等待著黎明，而當我醒來的時候，就會看到在光明裡的您的城市。

Things look phantastic in this dimness of the dusk — the spires whose bases are lost in the dark and tree tops like blots of ink. I shall wait for the morning and wake up to see thy city in the light.

321 /

神的靜默使人的思想成熟而成語言。

God's silence ripens man's thoughts into speech.

322 /

在我的一生裡，也有貧乏和沉默的地域。它們是我忙碌的日子得到陽光與空氣的幾片空曠之地。

There are tracts in my life that are bare and silent. They are the open spaces where my busy days had their light and air.

323 /

今天晚上棕櫚葉在嚓嚓地作響，海上有大浪，滿月
呵，就像世界在心脈悸跳。從哪個不可知的天空，
您在您的沉默裡帶來了愛的痛苦祕密？

Tonight there is a stir among the palm leaves, a swell in the
sea, Full Moon, like the heart throb of the world. From what
unknown sky hast thou carried in thy silence the aching
secret of love?

324 /

愛會消失──這乃是我們不能夠當作真理來接受的
一個事實。

That love can ever lose is a fact that we cannot accept as
truth.

325 /

「我相信你的愛。」讓這句話作我最後的話。
Let this be my last word, that I trust thy love.

新月集

The Crescent Moon

《新月集》有不可測的魔力

　　我對於太戈爾的詩最初發生濃厚的興趣，是在第一次讀《新月集》的時候。那時離現在將近五年，許地山君坐在我家的客廳裡，長髮垂到兩肩，在黃昏的微光中對我談到太戈爾的事。

　　他說，他在緬甸時，看到太戈爾的畫像，又聽人講到他，便買了他的詩集來讀。過了幾天，我到許地山君的宿舍裡去。他說：「我拿一本太戈爾的詩選送給你。」他便到書架上去找那本詩集。我立在窗前，四圍靜悄悄的，只有水池中噴泉的潺潺的聲音。我很寂靜地在等候讀那美麗的書。他不久便從書架上取下很小的一本綠紙面的書來。他說：「這是一個日本人選的太戈爾詩，你先拿去看看。太戈爾不多幾時前曾到過日本。」

　　我坐了車回家，在歸途中，借著新月與市燈的微光，約略地把它翻看了一遍。最使我喜歡的是它當中所選的幾首《新月集》的詩。那一夜，在燈下又看了一次。第二天，地山見我時，問道：「你最喜歡哪幾首？」我說：「《新月集》的幾首。」他隔了幾天，又拿了一本很美麗的書給我，他說：「這就是《新月集》。」從那時後，《新月集》便常在我的書桌上。直到現在，我還時時把它翻開來讀。

　　我譯《新月集》，也是受地山君的鼓勵。有一天，他把他所譯的《吉檀迦利》的幾首詩給我看，都是用古文譯的。我說：「譯得很好，但似乎太古奧了。」他說：「這一類的詩，應該用古奧的文體譯。至於《新月集》，卻又須用新妍流暢的文字譯。我想譯《吉檀迦利》，你為何不譯《新月集》呢？」於是我與他約，我們同時動手譯這兩部書。此後二年中，他的《吉檀迦利》固未譯成，我的《新月集》也時譯時輟。直至《小說月報》改革後，我才把自己所譯的《新月集》在它上面發表了幾首。地山譯的《吉檀迦利》卻始終沒有再譯下去，已譯的幾首也始終不肯拿出來發表。許多朋友卻時時地催我把這個工作做完。那時我正有選譯太戈爾詩的計畫，便一方面把舊譯稿整理一下，一方面又新譯了八九首出來，結果便成了現在的這個譯本。

　　我喜歡《新月集》，如我之喜歡安徒生的童話。安徒生的文字美麗而富有詩趣，他有一種不可測的魔力，能把我們帶到美麗和平的花的世界、蟲的世界、人魚的世界裡去；能使我們隨了他走進有靜的方池的綠水，有美的掛在黃昏的天空的雨後弧虹等等的天國裡去。《新月集》也具有這種不可測的魔力。它把我們從懷疑貪婪的罪惡的世界，帶到秀嫩天真的兒童的新月之國裡去。它能使我們重又回到坐在泥土裡以枯枝斷梗為戲的時代；它能使我們在心裡重溫著在海濱以貝殼為餐具、以落葉為舟、以綠草上的露點為圓珠的兒童的夢。總之，我們只要一翻開它來，便立刻如得到兩隻有魔術的翼膀，可以使自己飛翔到美靜天真的兒童國裡去。而這個兒童的天國便是作者的一個理想國。

我應該向許地山君表示謝意。他除了鼓勵我以外，在這個譯本寫好時，還曾為我校讀了一次。

鄭振鐸
一九二三年八月二十二日

《新月集》譯本出版後，曾承幾位朋友批評，這裡我要對他們表白十二分的謝意。現在乘再版的機會，把第一版中所有錯誤，就所能覺察到的，改正一下。讀者諸君及朋友們如果更有所發現，希望能夠告訴我，俾得於第三版時再校正。

鄭振鐸
一九二四年三月二十日

我在一九二三年的時候，曾把太戈爾的《新月集》譯為中文出版。但在那個譯本裡，並沒有把這部詩集完全譯出。這部詩集的英文本共有詩四十首，我只譯出了三十一首。現在把我的譯本重行校讀了一下，重譯並改正了不少地方，同時，並把沒有譯出的九首也補譯了出來。這可算是《新月集》的一部比較完整的譯本了。

　　應該在這裡謝謝孫家晉同志，他花了好幾天的工夫，把我的譯文仔細地校讀了一遍，有好幾個地方是採用了他的譯法的。

鄭振鐸

一九五四年八月六日

家 庭 /

我獨自在橫跨過田地的路上走著,夕陽像一個守財奴
似的,正藏起它最後的金子。

白晝更加深沉地沒入黑暗之中,那已經收割了的孤寂
的田地,默默地躺在那裡。天空裡突然升起了一個男
孩子的尖銳的歌聲。他穿過看不見的黑暗,留下他的
歌聲的轍痕跨過黃昏的靜謐。

他的鄉村的家坐落在荒涼的邊上,在甘蔗田的後面,
躲藏在香蕉樹、瘦長的檳榔樹、椰子樹和深綠色的賈
克果樹的陰影裡。

我在星光下獨自走著的路上停留了一會兒,我看見黑
沉沉的大地展開在我的面前,用她的手臂擁抱著無量
數的家庭。在那些家庭裡有著搖籃和床鋪,母親們的
心和夜晚的燈,還有年輕輕的生命,他們滿心歡樂,
卻渾然不知這樣的歡樂對於世界的價值。

The Home /

I paced alone on the road across the field while the sunset was hiding its last gold like a miser.

The daylight sank deeper and deeper into the darkness, and the widowed land, whose harvest had been reaped, lay silent. Suddenly a boy's shrill voice rose into the sky. He traversed the dark unseen, leaving the track of his song across the hush of the evening.

His village home lay there at the end of the waste land, beyond the sugar-cane field, hidden among the shadows of the banana and the slender areca palm, the cocoa-nut and the dark green jack-fruit trees.

I stopped for a moment in my lonely way under the starlight, and saw spread before me the darkened earth surrounding with her arms countless homes furnished with cradles and beds, mothers' hearts and evening lamps, and young lives glad with a gladness that knows nothing of its value for the world.

129

海 邊 /

孩子們匯集在無邊無際的世界的海邊。

無垠的天穹靜止地臨於頭上，不息的海水在足下洶湧。

孩子們匯集在無邊無際的世界的海邊，叫著，跳著。

他們拿沙來建築房屋，拿貝殼來做遊戲。他們把落葉編成了船，笑嘻嘻地把它們放到大海上。孩子們在世界的海邊，做他們的遊戲。

他們不知道怎樣泅水，他們不知道怎樣撒網。採珠的人為了珠潛水，商人們在他們的船上航行，孩子們卻只把小圓石聚了又散。他們不搜求寶藏；他們不知道怎樣撒網。

大海嘩笑著湧起波浪，而海灘的微笑蕩漾著淡淡的光
芒。致人死命的波濤，對著孩子們唱無意義的歌曲，
就像一個母親在搖動她孩子的搖籃時一樣。大海和孩
子們一同遊戲，而海灘的微笑蕩漾著淡淡的光芒。

孩子們匯集在無邊無際的世界的海邊。狂風暴雨飄遊
在無轍跡的天空上，航船沉醉在無轍跡的海水裡，死
正在外面活動，孩子們卻在遊戲。在無邊無際的世界
的海邊，孩子們大匯集著。

On the Seashore /

On the seashore of endless worlds children meet.
The infinite sky is motionless overhead and the restless water
is boisterous. On the seashore of endless worlds the children
meet with shouts and dances.

They build their houses with sand, and they play with empty
shells. With withered leaves they weave their boats and
smilingly float them on the vast deep. Children have their
play on the seashore of worlds.
They know not how to swim, they know not how to cast
nets. Pearl-fishers dive for pearls, merchants sail in their
ships, while children gather pebbles and scatter them again.
They seek not for hidden treasures, they know not how to
cast nets.

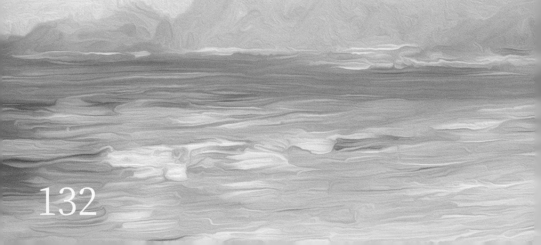

The sea surges up with laughter, and pale gleams the smile of the sea-beach. Death-dealing waves sing meaningless ballads to the children, even like a mother while rocking her baby's cradle. The sea plays with children, and pale gleams the smile of the sea-beach.

On the seashore of endless world children meet. Tempest roams in the pathless sky, ships are wrecked in the trackless water, death is abroad and children play. On the seashore of endless worlds is the great meeting of children.

133

來　源 /

流泛在孩子兩眼的睡眠 —— 有誰知道它是從什麼地方來的？是的，有個謠傳，說它是住在螢火蟲朦朧地照耀著林蔭的仙村裡，在那個地方，掛著兩個迷人的膽怯的蓓蕾。它便是從那個地方來吻了孩子的兩眼的。

當孩子睡時，在他唇上浮動著的微笑 —— 有誰知道它是從什麼地方生出來的？是的，有個謠傳，說新月的一線年輕的清光，觸著將消未消的秋雲邊上，於是微笑便初生在一個浴在清露裡的早晨的夢中了 —— 當孩子睡時，微笑便在他的唇上浮動著。

甜蜜柔嫩的新鮮生氣，像花一般地在孩子的四肢上開放著 —— 有誰知道它在什麼地方藏得這樣久？是的，當媽媽還是少女的時候，它已在愛的溫柔而沉靜的神祕中，潛伏在她的心裡了 —— 甜蜜柔嫩的新鮮生氣，像花一般地在孩子的四肢上開放著。

The Source /

The sleep that flits on baby's eyes — does anybody know from where it comes? Yes, there is a rumour that it has its dwelling where, in the fairy village among shadows of the forest dimly lit with glow-worms, there hang two shy buds of enchantment. From there it comes to kiss baby's eyes.

The smile that flickers on baby's lips when he sleeps — does anybody know where it was born? Yes, there is a rumour that a young pale beam of a crescent moon touched the edge of a vanishing autumn cloud, and there the smile was first born in the dream of a dew-washed morning — the smile that flickers on baby's lips when he sleeps.

The sweet, soft freshness that blooms on baby's limbs — does anybody know where it was hidden so long? Yes, when the mother was a young girl it lay pervading her heart in tender and silent mystery of love — the sweet, soft freshness that has bloomed on baby's limbs.

孩 童 之 道 /

只要孩子願意，他此刻便可飛上天去。
他所以不離開我們，並不是沒有緣故。
他愛把他的頭倚在媽媽的胸間，他即使是一刻不見她，
也是不行的。

孩子知道各式各樣的聰明話，雖然世間的人很少懂得
這些話的意義。
他所以永不想說，並不是沒有緣故。
他所要做的一件事，就是要學習從媽媽的嘴唇裡說出
來的話。那就是他所以看來這樣天真的緣故。

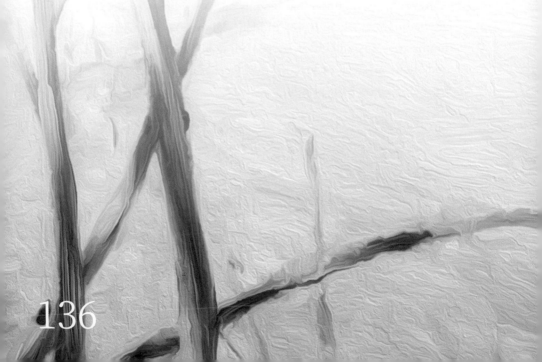

孩子有成堆的黃金與珠子，但他到這個世界上來，卻
像一個乞丐。
他所以這樣假裝了來，並不是沒有緣故。
這個可愛的小小的裸著身體的乞丐，所以假裝著完全
無助的樣子，便是想要乞求媽媽的愛的財富。

孩子在纖小的新月的世界裡，是一切束縛都沒有的。
他所以放棄了他的自由，並不是沒有緣故。
他知道有無窮的快樂藏在媽媽的心的小小一隅裡，被
媽媽親愛的手臂所擁抱，其甜美遠勝過自由。

孩子永不知道如何哭泣。他所住的是完全的樂土。
他所以要流淚，並不是沒有緣故。
雖然他用了可愛臉兒上的微笑，引逗得他媽媽熱切的
心向著他，然而他因為細故而發的小小哭聲，卻編成
了憐與愛的雙重約束的帶子。

Baby's Way /

If baby only wanted to, he could fly up to heaven this
moment.
It is not for nothing that he does not leave us.
He loves to rest his head on mother's bosom, and cannot ever
bear to lose sight of her.

Baby knows all manner of wise words, though few on earth
can understand their meaning.
It is not for nothing that he never wants to speak.
The one thing he wants is to learn mother's words from
mother's lips. That is why he looks so innocent.

Baby had a heap of gold and pearls, yet he came like a beggar
on to this earth.
It is not for nothing he came in such a disguise.

This dear little naked mendicant pretends to be utterly helpless, so that he may beg for mother's wealth of love.

Baby was so free from every tie in the land of the tiny crescent moon.
It was not for nothing he gave up his freedom.
He knows that there is room for endless joy in mother's little corner of a heart, and it is sweeter far than liberty to be caught and pressed in her dear arms.

Baby never knew how to cry. He dwelt in the land of perfect bliss.
It is not for nothing he has chosen to shed tears.
Though with the smile of his dear face he draws mother's yearning heart to him, yet his little cries over tiny troubles weave the double bond of pity and love.

不 被 注 意 的 花 飾 /

啊，誰給那件小外衫染上顏色的，我的孩子，誰使你
溫軟的肢體穿上那件紅的小外衫的？
你在早晨就跑出來到天井裡玩，你，跑著就像搖搖欲
跌似的。
但是誰給那件小外衫染上顏色的，我的孩子？

什麼事叫你大笑起來的，我的小小的命芽兒？
媽媽站在門邊，微笑地望著你。
她拍著她的雙手，她的手鐲叮噹地響著，你手裡拿著
你的竹竿在跳舞，活像一個小小的牧童。
但是什麼事叫你大笑起來的，我的小小的命芽兒？

喔，乞丐，你雙手攀摟住媽媽的頭頸，要乞討些什麼？
喔，貪得無厭的心，要我把整個世界從天上摘下來，
像摘一個果子似的，把它放在你的一雙小小的玫瑰色
的手掌上麼？
喔，乞丐，你要乞討些什麼？

140

風高興地帶走了你踝鈴的叮噹。

太陽微笑著，望著你的打扮。

當你睡在你媽媽的臂彎裡時，天空在上面望著你，而
早晨躡手躡腳地走到你的床跟前，吻著你的雙眼。

風高興地帶走了你踝鈴的叮噹。

仙鄉裡的夢婆飛過朦朧的天空，向你飛來。

在你媽媽的心頭上，那世界母親，正和你坐在一塊兒。

他，向星星奏樂的人，正拿著他的橫笛，站在你的窗
邊。

仙鄉裡的夢婆飛過朦朧的天空，向你飛來。

The Unheeded Pageant /

Ah, who was it coloured that little frock, my child, and covered your sweet limbs with that little red tunic?
You have come out in the morning to play in the courtyard, tottering and tumbling as you run.
But who was it coloured that little frock, my child?

What is it makes you laugh, my little life-bud?
Mother smiles at you standing on the threshold.
She claps her hands and her bracelets jingle, and you dance with your bamboo stick in your hand like a tiny little shepherd.
But what is it makes you laugh, my little life-bud?

O beggar, what do you beg for, clinging to your mother's neck with both your hands?
O greedy heart, shall I pluck the world like a fruit from the sky to place it on your little rosy palm?
O beggar, what are you begging for?

The wind carries away in glee the tinkling of your anklet bells.

The sun smiles and watches your toilet. The sky watches over you when you sleep in your mother's arms, and the morning comes tiptoe to your bed and kisses your eyes.

The wind carries away in glee the tinkling of your anklet bells.

The fairy mistress of dreams is coming towards you, flying through the twilight sky.

The world-mother keeps her seat by you in your mother's heart.

He who plays his music to the stars is standing at your window with his flute.

And the fairy mistress of dreams is coming towards you, flying through the twilight sky.

偷 睡 眠 者 /

誰從孩子的眼裡把睡眠偷了去呢？我一定要知道。

媽媽把她的水罐挾在腰間，走到近村汲水去了。

這是正午的時候，孩子們遊戲的時間已經過去了；池中的鴨子沉默無聲。

牧童躺在榕樹的蔭下睡著了。

白鶴莊重而安靜地立在檬果樹邊的泥澤裡。

就在這個時候，偷睡眠者跑來從孩子的兩眼裡捉住睡眠，便飛去了。

當媽媽回來時，她看見孩子四肢著地在屋裡爬著。

誰從孩子的眼裡把睡眠偷了去呢？我一定要知道。我一定要找到她，把她鎖起來。

我一定要向那個黑洞裡張望，在這個洞裡，有一道小泉從圓的和有皺紋的石上滴下來。

我一定要到醉花林中的沉寂的樹影裡搜尋，在這林中，鴿子在它們住的地方咕咕地叫著，仙女的腳環在繁星滿天的靜夜裡叮噹地響著。

我要在黃昏時，向靜靜的蕭蕭的竹林裡窺望，在這林
中，螢火蟲閃閃地耗費它們的光明，只要遇見一個人，
我便要問他：「誰能告訴我偷睡眠者住在什麼地方？」

誰從孩子的眼裡把睡眠偷了去呢？我一定要知道。
只要我能捉住她，怕不會給她一頓好教訓！
我要闖入她的巢穴，看她把所有偷來的睡眠藏在什麼
地方。

我要把它都奪來，帶回家去。
我要把她的雙翼縛得緊緊的，把她放在河邊，然後叫
她拿一根蘆葦在燈心草和睡蓮間釣魚為戲。

黃昏，街上已經收了市，村裡的孩子們都坐在媽媽的
膝上時，夜鳥便會譏笑地在她耳邊說：
「你現在還想偷誰的睡眠呢？」

Sleep-stealer /

Who stole sleep from baby's eyes? I must know.
Clasping her pitcher to her waist mother went to fetch water
from the village nearby.
It was noon. The children's playtime was over; the ducks in
the pond were silent.

The shepherd boy lay asleep under the shadow of the banyan
tree.
The crane stood grave and still in the swamp near the mango
grove.
In the meanwhile the Sleep-stealer came and, snatching sleep
from baby's eyes, flew away.
When mother came back she found baby travelling the room
over on all fours.

Who stole sleep from our baby's eyes? I must know. I must
find her and chain her up.
I must look into that dark cave, where, through boulders and
scowling stones, trickles a tiny stream.

I must search in the drowsy shade of the bakula grove, where
pigeons coo in their corner, and fairies' anklets tinkle in the
stillness of starry nights.

In the evening I will peep into the whispering silence of the bamboo forest, where fireflies squander their light, and will ask every creature I meet, "Can anybody tell me where the Sleep-stealer lives?"

Who stole sleep from baby's eyes? I must know.
Shouldn't I give her a good lesson if I could only catch her!
I would raid her nest and see where she hoards all her stolen sleep.

I would plunder it all, and carry it home.
I would bind her two wings securely, set her on the bank of the river, and then let her play at fishing with a reed among the rushes and water-lilies.

When the marketing is over in the evening, and the village children sit in their mothers' laps, then the night birds will mockingly din her ears with:
　"Whose sleep will you steal now?"

開　始　/

「我是從哪兒來的，你，在哪兒把我撿起來的？」孩子問他的媽媽說。

她把孩子緊緊地摟在胸前，半哭半笑地答道——

「你曾被我當作心願藏在我的心裡，我的寶貝。

「你曾存在於我孩童時代玩的泥娃娃身上；每天早晨我用泥土塑造我的神像，那時我反覆地塑了又捏碎了的就是你。

「你曾和我們的家庭守護神一同受到祀奉，我崇拜家神時也就崇拜了你。

「你曾活在我所有的希望和愛情裡、活在我的生命裡、我母親的生命裡。

「在主宰著我們家庭的不死精靈的膝上，你已經被撫育了好多代了。

「當我做女孩子的時候，我的心的花瓣兒張開，你就像一股花香似的散發出來。

「你的軟軟的溫柔，在我青春的肢體上開花了，像太陽出來之前的天空上的一片曙光。

「上天的第一寵兒，晨曦的孿生兄弟，你從世界的生命的溪流浮泛而下，終於停泊在我的心頭。

「當我凝視你的臉蛋的時候，神祕之感淹沒了我；你這屬於一切人的，竟成了我的。

「為了怕失掉你，我把你緊緊地摟在胸前。是什麼魔術把這世界的寶貝引到我這雙纖小的手臂裡來呢？」

149

The Beginning /

"Where have I come from, where did you pick me up?" the
baby asked its mother.
She answered half crying, half laughing, and clasping the
baby to her breast, —

"You were hidden in my heart as its desire, my darling.
You were in the dolls of my childhood's games; and when
with clay I made the image of my god every morning, I made
and unmade you then.
You were enshrined with our household deity, in his worship
I worshipped you.

In all my hopes and my loves, in my life, in the life of my
mother you have lived.
In the lap of the deathless Spirit who rules our home you
have been nursed for ages.

When in girlhood my heart was opening its petals, you hovered as a fragrance about it.
Your tender softness bloomed in my youthful limbs, like a glow in the sky before the sunrise.

Heaven's first darling, twin-born with the morning light, you have floated down the stream of the world's life, and at last you have stranded on my heart.

As I gaze on your face, mystery overwhelms me; you who belong to all have become mine.

For fear of losing you I hold you tight to my breast. What magic has snared the world's treasure in these slender arms of mine?"

孩 子 的 世 界 /

我願我能在我孩子自己的世界的中心，占一角清淨地。
我知道有星星同他說話，天空也在他面前垂下，用它
傻傻的雲朵和彩虹來娛悅他。

那些大家以為他是啞的人，那些看去像是永不會走動
的人，都帶了他們的故事，捧了滿裝著五顏六色的玩
具的盤子，匍匐地來到他的窗前。

我願我能在橫過孩子心中的道路上遊行，解脫了一切
的束縛；
在那兒，使者奉了無所謂的使命奔走於無史的諸王的
王國間；
在那兒，理智以她的法律造為紙鳶而飛放，真理也使
事實從桎梏中自由了。

Baby's World /

I wish I could take a quiet corner in the heart of my baby's very own world.
I know it has stars that talk to him, and a sky that stoops down to his face to amuse him with its silly clouds and rainbows.

Those who make believe to be dumb, and look as if they never could move, come creeping to his window with their stories and with trays crowded with bright toys.

I wish I could travel by the road that crosses baby's mind, and out beyond all bounds;
Where messengers run errands for no cause between the kingdoms of kings of no history;
Where Reason makes kites of her laws and flies them, and Truth sets Fact free from its fetters.

時 候 與 原 因 /

當我給你五顏六色的玩具的時候，我的孩子，我明白了為什麼雲上水上是這樣的色彩繽紛，為什麼花朵上染上絢爛的顏色的原因了——當我給你五顏六色的玩具的時候，我的孩子。

當我唱著使你跳舞的時候，我真的知道了為什麼樹葉兒響著音樂，為什麼波浪把它們的合唱的聲音送進靜聽著的大地的心頭的原因了——當我唱著使你跳舞的時候。

當我把糖果送到你貪得無厭的雙手上的時候，我知道了為什麼花萼裡會有蜜，為什麼水果裡會祕密地充溢了甜汁的原因了——當我把糖果送到你貪得無厭的雙手上的時候。

當我吻著你的臉蛋兒叫你微笑的時候，我的寶貝，我的確明白了在晨光裡從天上流下來的是什麼樣的快樂，而夏天的微颸吹拂在我的身體上的又是什麼樣的爽快——當我吻著你的臉蛋兒叫你微笑的時候。

When and Why /

When I bring you coloured toys, my child, I understand why there is such a play of colours on clouds, on water, and why flowers are painted in tints — when I give coloured toys to you, my child.

When I sing to make you dance, I truly know why there is music in leaves, and why waves send their chorus of voices to the heart of the listening earth — when I sing to make you dance.

When I bring sweet things to your greedy hands, I know why there is honey in the cup of the flower, and why fruits are secretly filled with sweet juice — when I bring sweet things to your greedy hands.

When I kiss your face to make you smile, my darling, I surely understand what pleasure streams from the sky in morning light, and what delight the summer breeze brings to my body — when I kiss you to make you smile.

責　備 /

為什麼你眼裡有了眼淚，我的孩子？

他們真是可怕，常常無謂地責備你！

你寫字時墨水玷汙了你的手和臉—— 這就是他們所以罵你醃臢的緣故麼？

呵，呸！他們也敢因為圓圓的月兒用墨水塗了臉，便罵它醃臢麼？

他們總要為了每一件小事去責備你，我的孩子。他們總是無謂地尋人錯處。

你遊戲時扯破了你的衣服—— 這就是他們所以說你不整潔的緣故麼？

呵，呸！秋之晨從破碎的雲衣中露出微笑，那麼，他們要叫它什麼呢？

他們對你說什麼話，儘管可以不去理睬他，我的孩子。

他們把你做錯的事長長地記了一筆帳。

誰都知道你是十分喜歡糖果的—— 這就是他們所以稱你做貪婪的緣故麼？

呵，呸！我們是喜歡你的，那麼，他們要叫我們幹什麼呢？

Defamation /

Why are those tears in your eyes, my child?
How horrid of them to be always scolding you for nothing!
You have stained your fingers and face with ink while writing
— is that why they call you dirty?
O, fie! Would they dare to call the full moon dirty because it
has smudged its face with ink?

For every little trifle they blame you, my child. They are
ready to find fault for nothing.
You tore your clothes while playing — is that why they call
you untidy?
O, fie! What would they call an autumn morning that smiles
through its ragged clouds?

Take no heed of what they say to you, my child.
They make a long list of your misdeeds. Everybody knows
how you love sweet things — is that why they call you
greedy?
O, fie! What then would they call us who love you?

審 判 官 /

你想說他什麼儘管說罷，但是我知道我孩子的短處。

我愛他並不因為他好，只是因為他是我的小小的孩子。

你如果把他的好處與壞處兩兩相權一下，恐怕你就會知道他是如何的可愛罷？

當我必須責罰他的時候，他更成為我的生命的一部分了。

當我使他眼淚流出時，我的心也和他同哭了。

只有我才有權去罵他，去責罰他，因為只有熱愛人的才可以懲戒人。

The Judge /

Say of him what you please, but I know my child's failings.
I do not love him because he is good, but because he is my
little child.

How should you know how dear he can be when you try to
weigh his merits against his faults?

When I must punish him he becomes all the more a part of
my being.
When I cause his tears to come my heart weeps with him.

I alone have a right to blame and punish, for he only may
chastise who loves.

玩　具　/

孩子，你真是快活呀，一早晨坐在泥土裡，耍著折下來的小樹枝兒。
我微笑地看你在那裡耍著那根折下來的小樹枝兒。
我正忙著算帳，一小時一小時在那裡加疊數字。

也許你在看我，想道：「這種好沒趣的遊戲，竟把你的一早晨的好時間浪費掉了！」
孩子，我忘了聚精會神玩耍樹枝與泥餅的方法了。
我尋求貴重的玩具，收集金塊與銀塊。

你呢，無論找到什麼，便去做你的快樂的遊戲，我呢，卻把我的時間與力氣都浪費在那些我永不能得到的東西上。
我在我的脆薄的獨木船裡掙扎著要航過欲望之海，竟忘了我也是在那裡做遊戲了。

Playthings /

Child, how happy you are sitting in the dust, playing with a broken twig all the morning.
I smile at your play with that little bit of a broken twig.
I am busy with my accounts, adding up figures by the hour.

Perhaps you glance at me and think, "What a stupid game to spoil your morning with!"
Child, I have forgotten the art of being absorbed in sticks and mud-pies.
I seek out costly playthings, and gather lumps of gold and silver.

With whatever you find you create your glad games, I spend both my time and my strength over things I never can obtain.
In my frail canoe I struggle to cross the sea of desire, and forget that I too am playing a game.

天 文 家 /

我不過說：「當傍晚圓圓的滿月掛在迦曇波的枝頭時，有人能去捉住它麼？」
哥哥卻對我笑道：「孩子呀，你真是我所見過最傻的孩子。月亮離我們這樣遠，誰能去捉住它呢？」

我說：「哥哥，你真傻！當媽媽向窗外探望，微笑著往下看我們遊戲時，你也能說她遠麼？」
哥哥還是說：「你這個傻孩子！但是，孩子，你到哪裡去找一個大得能抓住月亮的網呢？」

我說：「你自然可以用雙手去捉住它呀。」
但是哥哥還是笑著說：「你真是我所見過最傻的孩子！如果月亮走近了，你便知道它是多麼大了。」

我說：「哥哥，你們學校裡所教的，真是沒有用呀！當媽媽低下臉兒跟我們親嘴時，她的臉看來也是很大的麼？」
但是哥哥還是說：「你真是一個傻孩子。」

The Astronomer /

I only said, "When in the evening the round full moon gets entangled among the branches of that Kadam tree, couldn't somebody catch it?"
But dada [elder brother] laughed at me and said, "Baby, you are the silliest child I have ever known. The moon is ever so far from us, how could anybody catch it?"

I said, "Dada how foolish you are! When mother looks out of her window and smiles down at us playing, would you call her far away?"
Still dada said, "You are a stupid child! But, baby, where could you find a net big enough to catch the moon with?"

I said, "Surely you could catch it with your hands."
But dada laughed and said, "You are the silliest child I have known. If it came nearer, you would see how big the moon is."

I said, "Dada, what nonsense they teach at your school! When mother bends her face down to kiss us does her face look very big?"
But still dada says, "You are a stupid child."

163

雲 與 波 /

媽媽，住在雲端的人對我喚道——
「我們從醒的時候遊戲到白日終止。我們與黃金色的
曙光遊戲，我們與銀白色的月亮遊戲。」

我問道：「但是，我怎麼能夠上你那裡去呢？」
他們答道：「你到地球的邊上來，舉手向天，就可以
被接到雲端裡來了。」
「我媽媽在家裡等我呢，」我說，「我怎麼能離開她
而來呢？」
於是他們微笑著浮游而去。

但是我知道一件比這個更好的遊戲，媽媽。
我做雲，你做月亮。
我用兩隻手遮蓋你，我們的屋頂就是青碧的天空。

住在波浪上的人對我喚道——

「我們從早晨唱歌到晚上；我們前進又前進地旅行，

也不知我們所經過的是什麼地方。」

我問道：「但是，我怎麼能加入你們隊伍裡去呢？」

他們告訴我說：「來到岸旁，站在那裡，緊閉你的兩眼，

你就被帶到波浪上來了。」

我說：「傍晚的時候，我媽媽常要我在家裡 —— 我怎

麼能離開她而去呢！」

於是他們微笑著，跳著舞奔流過去。

但是我知道一件比這個更好的遊戲。

我是波浪，你是陌生的岸。

我奔流而進，進，進，笑哈哈地撞碎在你的膝上。

世界上就沒有一個人會知道我們倆在什麼地方。

Clouds and Waves /

Mother, the folk who live up in the clouds call out to me —
  "We play from the time we wake till the day ends. We play
with the golden dawn, we play with the silver moon."

I ask, "But, how am I to get up to you?"
They answer, "Come to the edge of the earth, lift up your
hands to the sky, and you will be taken up into the clouds."
  "My mother is waiting for me at home," I say. "How can
I leave her and come?"
Then they smile and float away.

But I know a nicer game than that, mother.
I shall be the cloud and you the moon.
I shall cover you with both my hands, and our house-top will
be the blue sky.

The folk who live in the waves call out to me —
　"We sing from morning till night; on and on we travel and know not where we pass."
I ask, "But, how am I to join you?"

They tell me, "Come to the edge of the shore and stand with your eyes tight shut, and you will be carried out upon the waves."
I say, "My mother always wants me at home in the evening — how can I leave her and go?"
Then they smile, dance and pass by.

But I know a better game than that.
I will be the waves and you will be a strange shore.
I shall roll on and on and on, and break upon your lap with laughter.
And no one in the world will know where we both are.

金 色 花 /

假如我變成了一朵金色花，只是為了好玩，長在那棵
樹的高枝上，笑哈哈地在風中搖擺，又在新生的樹葉
上跳舞，媽媽，你會認識我麼？

你要是叫道：「孩子，你在哪裡呀？」我暗暗地在那
裡匿笑，卻一聲兒不響。我要悄悄地開放花瓣兒，看
著你工作。

當你沐浴後，溼髮披在兩肩，穿過金色花的林蔭，走
到你做禱告的小庭院時，你會嗅到這花的香氣，卻不
知道這香氣是從我身上來的。

當你吃過中飯，坐在窗前讀《羅摩衍那》，那棵樹的
陰影落在你的頭髮與膝上時，我便要投我的小小的影
子在你的書頁上，正投在你所讀的地方。
但是你會猜得出這就是你的小孩子的小影子麼？

當你黃昏時拿了燈到牛棚裡去，我便要突然地再落到
地上來，又成了你的孩子，求你講個故事給我聽。

「你到哪裡去了，你這壞孩子？」
「我不告訴你，媽媽。」這就是你同我那時所要說的
話了。

The Champa Flower /

Supposing I became a champa flower, just for fun, and grew on a branch high up that tree, and shook in the wind with laughter and danced upon the newly budded leaves, would you know me, mother?

You would call, "Baby, where are you?" and I should laugh to myself and keep quite quiet.
I should slyly open my petals and watch you at your work.

When after your bath, with wet hair spread on your shoulders, you walked through the shadow of the champa tree to the little court where you say your prayers, you would notice the scent of the flower, but not know that it came from me.

When after the midday meal you sat at the window reading Ramayana, and the tree's shadow fell over your hair and your lap, I should fling my wee little shadow on to the page of your book, just where you were reading.

But would you guess that it was the tiny shadow of your little child?

When in the evening you went to the cowshed with the lighted lamp in your hand, I should suddenly drop on to the earth again and be your own baby once more, and beg you to tell me a story.

"Where have you been, you naughty child?"

"I won't tell you, mother." That's what you and I would say then.

仙 人 世 界 /

如果人們知道了我的國王的宮殿在哪裡，它就會消失
在空氣中的。
牆壁是白色的銀，屋頂是耀眼的黃金。
皇后住在有七個庭院的宮苑裡；她戴的一串珠寶，值
得整整七個王國的全部財富。

不過，讓我悄悄地告訴你，媽媽，我的國王的宮殿究
竟在哪裡。
它就在我們陽臺的角上，在那栽著杜爾茜花的花盆放
著的地方。

公主躺在遠遠的隔著七個不可逾越的重洋的那一岸沉
睡著。
除了我自己，世界上便沒有人能夠找到她。
她臂上有鐲子，她耳上掛著珍珠，她的頭髮拖到地板
上。
當我用我的魔杖點觸她的時候，她就會醒過來，而當
她微笑時，珠玉將會從她唇邊落下來。

不過，讓我在你的耳朵邊悄悄地告訴你，媽媽，她就住在我們陽臺的角上，在那栽著杜爾茜花的花盆放著的地方。

當你要到河裡洗澡的時候，你走上屋頂的那座陽臺來罷。

我就坐在牆的陰影所聚會的一個角落裡。

我只讓小貓兒跟我在一起，因為它知道那故事裡的理髮匠住的地方。

不過，讓我在你的耳朵邊悄悄地告訴你，那故事裡的理髮匠到底住在哪裡。

他住的地方，就在陽臺的角上，在那栽著杜爾茜花的花盆放著的地方。

173

Fairyland /

If people came to know where my king's palace is, it would vanish into the air.
The walls are of white silver and the roof of shining gold.
The queen lives in a palace with seven courtyards, and she wears a jewel that cost all the wealth of seven kingdoms.

But, let me tell you, mother, in a whisper, where my king's palace is.
It is at the corner of our terrace where the pot of the tulsi plant stands.

The princess lies sleeping on the far-away shore of the seven impassable seas.
There is none in the world who can find her but myself.
She has bracelets on her arms and pearl drops in her ears; her hair sweeps down upon the floor.
She will wake when I touch her with my magic wand, and jewels will fall from her lips when she smiles.

But let me whisper in your ear, mother; she is there in the corner of our terrace where the pot of the tulsi plant stands.

When it is time for you to go to the river for your bath, step up to that terrace on the roof.
I sit in the corner where the shadows of the walls meet together.
Only puss is allowed to come with me, for she knows where the barber in the story lives.

But let me whisper, mother, in your ear where the barber in the story lives.
It is at the corner of the terrace where the pot of the tulsi plant stands.

流 放 的 地 方 /

媽媽，天空上的光成了灰色了；我不知道是什麼時候了。
我玩得怪沒趣的，所以到你這裡來了。這是星期六，
是我們的休息日。
放下你的活計，媽媽，坐在靠窗的一邊，告訴我童話
裡的特潘塔沙漠在什麼地方？

雨的影子遮掩了整個白天。
凶猛的電光用它的爪子抓著天空。
當烏雲轟轟地響著，天打著雷的時候，我總愛心裡帶
著恐懼爬伏到你的身上。當大雨傾瀉在竹葉子上好幾
個鐘頭，而我們的窗戶為狂風震得格格發響的時候，
我就愛獨自和你坐在屋裡，媽媽，聽你講童話裡的特
潘塔沙漠的故事。

它在哪裡，媽媽，在哪一個海洋的岸上，在哪些個山
峰的腳下，在哪一個國王的國土裡？
田地上沒有此疆彼壤的界石，也沒有村人在黃昏時走
回家的，或婦人在樹林裡撿拾枯枝而捆載到市場上去
的道路。沙地上只有一小塊一小塊的黃色草地，只有
一株樹，就是那一對聰明的老鳥兒在那裡做窩的，那
個地方就是特潘塔沙漠。

我能夠想像得到，就在這樣一個烏雲密布的日子，國王的年輕的兒子，怎樣地獨自騎著一匹灰色馬，走過這個沙漠，去尋找那被囚禁在不可知的重洋之外的巨人宮裡的公主。

當雨霧在遙遠的天空下降，電光像一陣突然發作的痛楚的痙攣似的閃射的時候，他可記得他不幸的母親，為國王所棄，正在掃除牛棚，眼裡流著眼淚，當他騎馬走過童話裡的特潘塔沙漠的時候？

看，媽媽，一天還沒有完，天色就差不多黑了，那邊村莊的路上沒有什麼旅客了。
牧童早就從牧場上回家了，人們都已從田地裡回來，坐在他們草屋的簷下的草席上，眼望著陰沉的雲塊。

媽媽，我把我所有的書本都放在書架上了 —— 不要叫我現在做功課。當我長大了，大得像爸爸一樣的時候，我將會學到必須學的東西的。但是，今天你可得告訴我，媽媽，童話裡的特潘塔沙漠在什麼地方？

The Land of the Exile /

Mother, the light has grown grey in the sky; I do not know what the time is.

There is no fun in my play, so I have come to you. It is Saturday, our holiday.

Leave off your work, mother; sit here by the window and tell me where the desert of Tepantar in the fairy tale is?

The shadow of the rains has covered the day from end to end.

The fierce lightning is scratching the sky with its nails.

When the clouds rumble and it thunders, I love to be afraid in my heart and cling to you. When the heavy rain patters for hours on the bamboo leaves, and our windows shake and rattle at the gusts of wind, I like to sit alone in the room, mother, with you, and hear you talk about the desert of Tepantar in the fairy tale.

Where is it, mother, on the shore of what sea, at the foot of what hills, in the kingdom of what king?

There are no hedges there to mark the fields, no footpath across it by which the villagers reach their village in the evening, or the woman who gathers dry sticks in the forest can bring her load to the market. With patches of yellow grass in the sand and only one tree where the pair of wise old birds have their nest, lies the desert of Tepantar.

I can imagine how, on just such a cloudy day, the young son of the king is riding alone on a grey horse through the desert, in search of the princess who lies imprisoned in the giant's palace across that unknown water.

When the haze of the rain comes down in the distant sky, and lightning starts up like a sudden fit of pain, does he remember his unhappy mother, abandoned by the king, sweeping the cow-stall and wiping her eyes, while he rides through the desert of Tepantar in the fairy tale?

See, mother, it is almost dark before the day is over, and there are no travellers yonder on the village road.
The shepherd boy has gone home early from the pasture, and men have left their fields to sit on mats under the eaves of their huts, watching the scowling clouds.

Mother, I have left all my books on the shelf — do not ask me to do my lessons now.
When I grow up and am big like my father, I shall learn all that must be learnt. But just for today, tell me, mother, where the desert of Tepantar in the fairy tale is?

179

雨 天 /

烏雲很快地集攏在森林的黝黑的邊緣上。

孩子,不要出去呀!

湖邊的一行棕樹,向暝暗的天空撞著頭;羽毛零亂的
烏鴉,靜悄悄地棲在羅望子的枝上,河的東岸正被烏
沉沉的暝色所侵襲。

我們的牛繫在籬上,高聲鳴叫。

孩子,在這裡等著,等我先把牛牽進牛棚裡去。

許多人都擠在池水泛溢的田間,捉那從泛溢的池中逃
出來的魚兒,雨水成了小河,流過狹弄,好像一個嬉
笑的孩子從他媽媽那裡跑開,故意要惱她一樣。

180

聽呀，有人在淺灘上喊船夫呢。

孩子，天色暝暗了，渡頭的擺渡船已經停了。

天空好像是在滂沱的雨上快跑著；河裡的水喧叫而且暴躁；婦人們早已拿著汲滿了水的水罐，從恆河畔匆匆地回家了。

夜裡用的燈，一定要預備好。

孩子，不要出去呀！

到市場去的大道已沒有人走，到河邊去的小路又很滑。

風在竹林裡咆哮著、掙扎著，好像一隻落在網中的野獸。

The Rainy Day /

Sullen clouds are gathering fast over the black fringe of the forest.
O child, do not go out!
The palm trees in a row by the lake are smiting their heads against the dismal sky; the crows with their draggled wings are silent on the tamarind branches, and the eastern bank of the river is haunted by a deepening gloom.

Our cow is lowing loud, tied at the fence.
O child, wait here till I bring her into the stall.
Men have crowded into the flooded field to catch the fishes as they escape from the overflowing ponds; the rain water is running in rills through the narrow lanes like a laughing boy who has run away from his mother to tease her.

Listen, someone is shouting for the boatman at the ford.

O child, the daylight is dim, and the crossing at the ferry is closed.

The sky seems to ride fast upon the madly-rushing rain; the water in the river is loud and impatient; women have hastened home early from the Ganges with their filled pitchers.

The evening lamps must be made ready.

O child, do not go out!

The road to the market is desolate, the lane to the river is slippery. The wind is roaring and struggling among the bamboo branches like a wild beast tangled in a net.

紙 船 /

我每天把紙船一艘艘放在急流的溪中。
我用大黑字寫我的名字和我住的村名在紙船上。
我希望住在異地的人會得到這紙船，知道我是誰。

我把園中長的秀利花載在我的小船上，希望這些黎明
開的花能在夜裡被平平安安地帶到岸上。
我投我的紙船到水裡，仰望天空，看見小朵的雲正張
著滿鼓著風的白帆。

我不知道天上有我的什麼遊伴把這些船放下來同我的
船比賽！
夜來了，我的臉埋在手臂裡，夢見我的紙船在子夜的
星光下緩緩地浮泛前去。
睡仙坐在船裡，帶著滿載著夢的籃子。

Paper Boats /

Day by day I float my paper boats one by one down the running stream.
In big black letters I write my name on them and the name of the village where I live.
I hope that someone in some strange land will find them and know who I am.

I load my little boats with shiuli flowers from our garden, and hope that these blooms of the dawn will be carried safely to land in the night.
I launch my paper boats and look up into the sky and see the little clouds setting their white bulging sails.

I know not what playmate of mine in the sky sends them down the air to race with my boats!
When night comes I bury my face in my arms and dream that my paper boats float on and on under the midnight stars.
The fairies of sleep are sailing in them, and the lading is their baskets full of dreams.

185

水 手 /

船夫曼特胡的船隻停泊在拉琪根琪碼頭。

這隻船無用地裝載著黃麻，無所事事地停泊在那裡已
經好久了。

只要他肯把他的船借給我，我就給它安裝一百支槳，
揚起五個或六個或七個布帆來。

我絕不把它駕駛到愚蠢的市場上去。

我將航行遍仙人世界裡的七個大海和十三條河道。

但是，媽媽，你不要躲在角落裡為我哭泣。

我不會像羅摩犍陀羅那樣，到森林中去，一去十四年
才回來。

我將成為故事中的王子，把我的船裝滿我所喜歡的東西。

我將帶我的朋友阿細和我做伴，我們要快快樂樂地航行於仙人世界裡的七個大海和十三條河道。

我將在絕早的晨光裡張帆航行。

中午，你正在池塘裡洗澡的時候，我們將在一個陌生的國王的國土上了。我們將經過特浦尼淺灘，把特潘塔沙漠拋落在我們的後面。

當我們回來的時候，天色快黑了，我將告訴你我們所見到的一切。

我將越過仙人世界裡的七個大海和十三條河道。

The Sailor /

The boat of the boatman Madhu is moored at the wharf of Rajgunj.
It is uselessly laden with jute, and has been lying there idle for ever so long.
If he would only lend me his boat, I should man her with a hundred oars, and hoist sails, five or six or seven.
I should never steer her to stupid markets. I should sail the seven seas and the thirteen rivers of fairyland.

But, mother, you won't weep for me in a corner.
I am not going into the forest like Ramachandra to come back only after fourteen years.

I shall become the prince of the story, and fill my boat with whatever I like.

I shall take my friend Ashu with me. We shall sail merrily across the seven seas and the thirteen rivers of fairyland.

We shall set sail in the early morning light. When at noontide you are bathing at the pond, we shall be in the land of a strange king.

We shall pass the ford of Tirpurni, and leave behind us the desert of Tepantar.

When we come back it will be getting dark, and I shall tell you of all that we have seen.

I shall cross the seven seas and the thirteen rivers of fairyland.

189

對　岸　/

我渴想到河的對岸去。

在那邊，好些船隻一排繫在竹竿上；人們在早晨乘船
渡過那邊去，肩上扛著犁頭，去耕耘他們遠處的田；
在那邊，牧人使他們鳴叫著的牛游泳到河旁的牧場去；
黃昏的時候，他們都回家了，只留下豺狼在這滿長著
野草的島上哀叫。

媽媽，如果你不在意，我長大的時候，要做這渡船的
船夫。

據說有好些古怪的池塘藏在這個高岸之後。

雨過去了，一群一群的野鶩飛到那裡去，茂盛的蘆葦
在岸邊四圍生長，水鳥在那裡生蛋；竹雞帶著跳舞的
尾巴，將它們細小的足印印在潔淨的軟泥上；黃昏的
時候，長草頂著白花，邀月光在長草的波浪上浮游。

媽媽，如果你不在意，我長大的時候，要做這渡船的
船夫。

我要自此岸到彼岸，渡過來，渡過去，所有村中正在
那兒沐浴的男孩女孩，都要詫異地望著我。
太陽升到中天，早晨變為正午了，我將跑到你那裡去，
說道：「媽媽，我餓了！」

一天完了，影子俯伏在樹底下，我便要在黃昏中回家
來。
我將永不同爸爸那樣，離開你到城裡去做事。
媽媽，如果你不在意，我長大的時候，要做這渡船的
船夫。

The Further Bank /

I long to go over there to the further bank of the river,
Where those boats are tied to the bamboo poles in a line;
Where men cross over in their boats in the morning with
ploughs on their shoulders to till their far-away fields;
Where the cowherds make their lowing cattle swim across to
the riverside pasture;
Whence they all come back home in the evening, leaving the
jackals to howl in the island overgrown with weeds.
Mother, if you don't mind, I should like to become the
boatman of the ferry when I am grown up.

They say there are strange pools hidden behind that high
bank.
Where flocks of wild ducks come when the rains are over,
and thick reeds grow round the margins where waterbirds lay
their eggs;
Where snipes with their dancing tails stamp their tiny
footprints upon the clean soft mud;
Where in the evening the tall grasses crested with white
flowers invite the moonbeam to float upon their waves.

Mother, if you don't mind, I should like to become the boatman of the ferryboat when I am grown up.

I shall cross and cross back from bank to bank, and all the boys and girls of the village will wonder at me while they are bathing.

When the sun climbs the mid sky and morning wears on to noon, I shall come running to you, saying, "Mother, I am hungry!"

When the day is done and the shadows cower under the trees, I shall come back in the dusk.

I shall never go away from you into the town to work like father.

Mother, if you don't mind, I should like to become the boatman of the ferryboat when I am grown up.

花 的 學 校 /

當雷雲在天上轟響，六月的陣雨落下的時候，
潤溼的東風走過荒野，在竹林中吹著口笛。
於是一群一群的花從無人知道的地方突然跑出來，在
綠草上狂歡地跳著舞。

媽媽，我真的覺得那群花朵是在地下的學校裡上學。
他們關了門做功課，如果他們想在散學以前出來遊戲，
他們的老師是要罰他們站壁角的。

雨一來，他們便放假了。
樹枝在林中互相碰觸著，綠葉在狂風裡蕭蕭地響著，

雷雲拍著大手，花孩子們便在那時候穿了紫的、黃的、
白的衣裳，衝了出來。

你可知道，媽媽，他們的家是在天上，在星星所住的
地方。
你沒有看見他們怎樣地急著要到那兒去麼？你不知道
他們為什麼那樣急急忙忙麼？

我自然能夠猜得出他們是對誰揚起雙臂來：他們也有
他們的媽媽，就像我有我自己的媽媽一樣。

The Flower-school /

When storm clouds rumble in the sky and June showers
come down,
The moist east wind comes marching over the heath to blow
its bagpipes among the bamboos.
Then crowds of flowers come out of a sudden, from nobody
knows where, and dance upon the grass in wild glee.

Mother, I really think the flowers go to school underground.
They do their lessons with doors shut, and if they want to
come out to play before it is time, their master makes them
stand in a corner.

When the rains come they have their holidays.
Branches clash together in the forest, and the leaves rustle in
the wild wind, the thunder-clouds clap their giant hands and

the flower children rush out in dresses of pink and yellow and white.

Do you know, mother, their home is in the sky, where the stars are.
Haven't you seen how eager they are to get there? Don't you know why they are in such a hurry?

Of course, I can guess to whom they raise their arms: they have their mother as I have my own.

商 人 /

媽媽，讓我們想像，你待在家裡，我到異邦去旅行。
再想像，我的船已經裝得滿滿的在碼頭上等候啟碇了。
現在，媽媽，好生想一想再告訴我，回來的時候我要
帶些什麼給你。

媽媽，你要一堆一堆的黃金麼？
在金河的兩岸，田野裡全是金色的稻實。
在林蔭的路上，金色花也一朵一朵地落在地上。
我要為你把它們全都收拾起來，放在好幾百個籃子裡。

媽媽，你要秋天的雨點一般大的珍珠麼？

我要渡海到珍珠島的岸上去。

那個地方，在清晨的曙光裡，珠子在草地的野花上顫動，珠子落在綠草上，珠子被洶狂的海浪一大把一大把地撒在沙灘上。

我的哥哥呢，我要送他一對有翼的馬，會在雲端飛翔的。

爸爸呢，我要帶一支有魔力的筆給他，他還沒有察覺，筆就寫出字來了。

你呢，媽媽，我一定要把那個值七個王國的首飾箱和珠寶送給你。

The Merchant /

Imagine, mother, that you are to stay at home and I am to travel into strange lands.
Imagine that my boat is ready at the landing fully laden.
Now think well, mother, before you say what I shall bring for you when I come back.

Mother, do you want heaps and heaps of gold?
There, by the banks of golden streams, fields are full of golden harvest.
And in the shade of the forest path the golden champa flowers drop on the ground.
I will gather them all for you in many hundred baskets.

Mother, do you want pearls big as the raindrops of autumn?
I shall cross to the pearl island shore.

200

There in the early morning light pearls tremble on the meadow flowers, pearls drop on the grass, and pearls are scattered on the sand in spray by the wild sea-waves.

My brother shall have a pair of horses with wings to fly among the clouds.
For father I shall bring a magic pen that, without his knowing, will write of itself.
For you, mother, I must have the casket and jewel that cost seven kings their kingdoms.

同 情 /

如果我只是一隻小狗，而不是你的小孩，親愛的媽媽，
當我想吃你盤裡的東西時，你要向我說「不」麼？
你要趕開我，對我說道，「滾開，你這淘氣的小狗」
麼？
那麼，走吧，媽媽，走吧！當你叫喚我的時候，我就
永不到你那裡去，也永不要你再餵我吃東西了。

如果我只是一隻綠色的小鸚鵡，而不是你的小孩，親
愛的媽媽，你要把我緊緊地鎖住，怕我飛走麼？
你要對我搖你的手，說道，「真是不知感恩的賤鳥呀！
整夜盡在咬它的鏈子」麼？
那麼，走吧，媽媽，走吧！我要跑到樹林裡去；我就
永不再讓你抱我在你的臂彎裡了。

Sympathy /

If I were only a little puppy, not your baby, mother dear, would you say "No" to me if I tried to eat from your dish? Would you drive me off, saying to me, "Get away, you naughty little puppy?" Then go, mother, go! I will never come to you when you call me, and never let you feed me any more.

If I were only a little green parrot, and not your baby, mother dear, would you keep me chained lest I should fly away? Would you shake your finger at me and say, "What an ungrateful wretch of a bird! It is gnawing at its chain day and night?" Then, go, mother, go! I will run away into the woods; I will never let you take me in your arms again.

203

職　業 /

早晨，鐘敲十下的時候，我沿著我們的小巷到學校去。

每天我都遇見那個小販，他叫道：「鐲子呀，亮晶晶的鐲子！」

他沒有什麼事情急著要做，他沒有哪條街一定要走，他沒有什麼地方一定要去，他沒有什麼時間一定要回家。

我願意我是一個小販，在街上過日子，叫著：「鐲子呀，亮晶晶的鐲子！」

下午四點，我從學校裡回家。

從一家門口，我看得見一個園丁在那裡掘地。

他用他的鋤子，要怎麼掘，便怎麼掘，他被塵土汙了衣裳，如果他被太陽曬黑了或是身上被打溼了，都沒有人罵他。

我願意我是一個園丁,在花園裡掘地,誰也不來阻止我。

天色剛黑,媽媽就送我上床。
從開著的窗口,我看見更夫走來走去。
小巷又黑又冷清,路燈立在那裡,像一個頭上生著一隻紅眼睛的巨人。更夫搖著他的提燈,跟他身邊的影子一起走著,他一生一次都沒有上床去過。
我願意我是一個更夫,整夜在街上走,提了燈去追逐影子。

205

Vocation /

When the gong sounds ten in the morning and I walk to
school by our lane,
Every day I meet the hawker crying, "Bangles, crystal
bangles!"
There is nothing to hurry him on, there is no road he must
take, no place he must go to, no time when he must come
home.
I wish I were a hawker, spending my day in the road,
crying, "Bangles, crystal bangles!"

When at four in the afternoon I come back from the school,
I can see through the gate of that house the gardener digging
the ground.
He does what he likes with his spade, he soils his clothes with
dust, nobody takes him to task if he gets baked in the sun or
gets wet.
I wish I were a gardener digging away at the garden with
nobody to stop me from digging.

Just as it gets dark in the evening and my mother sends me to bed,

I can see through my open window the watchman walking up and down.

The lane is dark and lonely, and the street-lamp stands like a giant with one red eye in its head.

The watchman swings his lantern and walks with his shadow at his side, and never once goes to bed in his life.

I wish I were a watchman walking the streets all night, chasing the shadows with my lantern.

長 者 /

媽媽，你的孩子真傻！她是那麼可笑地不懂事！
她不知道路燈和星星的分別。
當我們玩著把小石子當食物的遊戲時，她便以為它們
真是吃的東西，竟想放進嘴裡去。

當我翻開一本書，放在她面前，在她讀 a，b，c 時，
她卻用手把書頁撕了，無端快活地叫起來，你的孩子
就是這樣做功課的。
當我生氣地對她搖頭，罵她，說她頑皮時，她卻哈哈
大笑，以為很有趣。

誰都知道爸爸不在家，但是，如果我在遊戲時高聲叫
一聲「爸爸」，她便要高興地四面張望，以為爸爸真
是近在身邊。

當我把洗衣人帶來載衣服回去的驢子當作學生，並且
警告她說，我是老師，她卻無緣無故地亂叫起我哥哥
來。

你的孩子要捉月亮。

她是這樣的可笑；她把格尼許喚作琪奴許。

媽媽，你的孩子真傻，她是那麼可笑地不懂事！

209

Superior /

Mother, your baby is silly! She is so absurdly childish!
She does not know the difference between the lights in the
streets and the stars.
When we play at eating with pebbles, she thinks they are real
food, and tries to put them into her mouth.

When I open a book before her and ask her to learn her a,
b, c, she tears the leaves with her hands and roars for joy at
nothing; this is your baby's way of doing her lesson.
When I shake my head at her in anger and scold her and call
her naughty, she laughs and thinks it great fun.

Everybody knows that father is away, but, if in play I call aloud "Father," she looks about her in excitement and thinks that father is near.
When I hold my class with the donkeys that our washerman brings to carry away the clothes and I warn her that I am the schoolmaster, she will scream for no reason and call me dada.

Your baby wants to catch the moon. She is so funny; she calls Ganesh Ganush.
Mother, your baby is silly, she is so absurdly childish!

小 大 人 /

我人很小，因為我是一個小孩子，到了我像爸爸一樣年紀時，便要變大了。

我的老師要是走來說道：「時候晚了，把你的石板、你的書拿來。」

我便要告訴他道：「你不知道我已經同爸爸一樣大了麼？我絕不再學什麼功課了。」

我的老師便將驚異地說道：「他讀書不讀書可以隨便，因為他是大人了。」

我將自己穿了衣裳，走到人群擁擠的市場裡去。

我的叔叔要是跑過來說道：「你要迷路了，我的孩子，讓我領著你罷。」

我便要回答道：「你沒有看見麼，叔叔，我已經同爸爸一樣大了？我決定要獨自一個人到市場裡去。」

叔叔便將說道：「是的，他隨便到哪裡去都可以，因為他是大人了。」

當我正拿錢給我的保母時，媽媽便要從浴室中出來，因為我是知道怎樣用我的鑰匙去開銀箱的。

媽媽要是說道：「你在做什麼呀，頑皮的孩子？」

我便要告訴她道：「媽媽，你不知道我已經同爸爸一樣大了麼？我必須拿錢給保母。」

媽媽便將自言自語道：「他可以隨便把錢給他所喜歡的人，因為他是大人了。」

當十月裡放假的時候，爸爸將要回家，他會以為我還是一個小孩子，為我從城裡帶了小鞋子和小綢衫來。

我便要說道：「爸爸，把這些東西給哥哥罷，因為我已經同你一樣大了。」

爸爸便將想了一想，說道：「他可以隨便去買他自己穿的衣裳，因為他是大人了。」

The Little Big Man /

I am small because I am a little child. I shall be big when I am as old as my father is.

My teacher will come and say, "It is late, bring your slate and your books."

I shall tell him, "Do you not know I am as big as father? And I must not have lessons any more."

My master will wonder and say, "He can leave his books if he likes, for he is grown up."

I shall dress myself and walk to the fair where the crowd is thick.

My uncle will come rushing up to me and say, "You will get lost, my boy; let me carry you."

I shall answer, "Can't you see, uncle, I am as big as father? I must go to the fair alone."

Uncle will say, "Yes, he can go wherever he likes, for he is grown up."

Mother will come from her bath when I am giving money to my nurse, for I shall know how to open the box with my key. Mother will say, "What are you about, naughty child?"

I shall tell her, "Mother, don't you know, I am as big as father, and I must give silver to my nurse."
Mother will say to herself, "He can give money to whom he likes, for he is grown up."

In the holiday time in October father will come home and, thinking that I am still a baby, will bring for me from the town little shoes and small silken frocks.
I shall say, "Father, give them to my dada, for I am as big as you are."

Father will think and say, "He can buy his own clothes if he likes, for he is grown up."

十 二 點 鐘 /

媽媽，我真想現在不做功課了。我整個早晨都在念書呢。

你說，現在還不過是十二點鐘。假定不會晚過十二點罷；難道你不能把不過是十二點鐘想像成下午麼？

我能夠容容易易地想像：現在太陽已經到了那片稻田的邊緣上了，老態龍鍾的漁婆正在池邊採擷香草做她的晚餐。

我閉上了眼就能夠想到，馬塔爾樹下的陰影是更深黑了，池塘裡的水看來黑得發亮。

假如十二點鐘能夠在黑夜裡來到，為什麼黑夜不能在十二點鐘的時候來到呢？

216

Twelve O'clock /

Mother, I do want to leave off my lessons now. I have been at my book all the morning.

You say it is only twelve o'clock. Suppose it isn't any later; can't you ever think it is afternoon when it is only twelve o'clock?

I can easily imagine now that the sun has reached the edge of that rice-field, and the old fisher-woman is gathering herbs for her supper by the side of the pond.

I can just shut my eyes and think that the shadows are growing darker under the madar tree, and the water in the pond looks shiny black.

If twelve o'clock can come in the night, why can't the night come when it is twelve o'clock?

著 作 家 /

你說爸爸寫了許多書，但我卻不懂得他所寫的東西。
他整個黃昏讀書給你聽，但是你真懂得他的意思麼？

媽媽，你給我們講的故事，真是好聽呀！我很奇怪，
爸爸為什麼不能寫那樣的書呢？
難道他從來沒有從他自己的媽媽那裡聽見過巨人和神
仙和公主的故事麼？
還是已經完全忘記了？

他常常耽誤了沐浴，你不得不走去叫他一百多次。
你總要等候著，把他的菜溫著等他，但他忘了，還儘
管寫下去。
爸爸老是以著書為遊戲。

如果我一走進爸爸房裡去遊戲，你就要走來叫道：「真
是一個頑皮的孩子！」

如果我稍微出一點聲音，你就要說：「你沒有看見你
爸爸正在工作麼？」
老是寫了又寫，有什麼趣味呢？

當我拿起爸爸的鋼筆或鉛筆，像他一模一樣地在他的
書上寫著，——a，b，c，d，e，f，g，h，i，——那時，
你為什麼跟我生氣呢，媽媽？
爸爸寫時，你卻從來不說一句話。

當我爸爸耗費了那麼一大堆紙時，媽媽，你似乎全不
在乎。
但是，如果我只取了一張紙去做一隻船，你卻要說：
「孩子，你真討厭！」
你對於爸爸拿黑點子塗滿了紙的兩面，汙損了許多許
多張紙，你心裡怎麼想呢？

Authorship /

You say that father writes a lot of books, but what he writes I don't understand.
He was reading to you all the evening, but could you really make out what he meant?

What nice stories, mother, you can tell us! Why can't father write like that, I wonder?
Did he never hear from his own mother stories of giants and fairies and princesses?
Has he forgotten them all?

Often when he gets late for his bath you have to go and call him a hundred times.
You wait and keep his dishes warm for him, but he goes on writing and forgets.
Father always plays at making books.

If ever I go to play in father's room, you come and call me, "what a naughty child!"
If I make the slightest noise, you say, "Don't you see that father's at his work?"
What's the fun of always writing and writing?

When I take up father's pen or pencil and write upon his book just as he does, — a, b, c, d, e, f, g, h, i, — why do you get cross with me, then, mother?
You never say a word when father writes.

When my father wastes such heaps of paper, mother, you don't seem to mind at all.
But if I take only one sheet to make a boat with, you say, "Child, how troublesome you are!"
What do you think of father's spoiling sheets and sheets of paper with black marks all over on both sides?

惡 郵 差 /

你為什麼坐在那邊地板上不言不動的，告訴我呀，親愛的媽媽？

雨從開著的窗口打進來了，把你身上全打溼了，你卻不管。

你聽見鐘已打四下了麼？正是哥哥從學校裡回家的時候了。

到底發生了什麼事，你的神色這樣不對？

你今天沒有接到爸爸的信麼？

我看見郵差在他的袋裡帶了許多信來，幾乎鎮裡的每個人都分送到了。

只有爸爸的信，他留起來給他自己看。我確信這個郵差是個壞人。

但是不要因此不樂呀，親愛的媽媽。

明天是鄰村市集的日子。你叫女僕去買些筆和紙來。
我自己會寫爸爸所寫的一切信，使你找不出一點錯處來。
我要從 A 字一直寫到 K 字。

但是，媽媽，你為什麼笑呢？
你不相信我能寫得同爸爸一樣好！

但是我將用心畫格子，把所有的字母都寫得又大又美。
當我寫好了時，你以為我也像爸爸那樣傻，把它投入
可怕的郵差的袋中麼？

我立刻就自己送來給你，而且一個字母一個字母地幫
你讀。
我知道那郵差是不肯把真正的好信送給你的。

The Wicked Postman /

Why do you sit there on the floor so quiet and silent, tell me, mother dear?
The rain is coming in through the open window, making you all wet, and you don't mind it.
Do you hear the gong striking four? It is time for my brother to come home from school.

What has happened to you that you look so strange?
Haven't you got a letter from father today?
I saw the postman bringing letters in his bag for almost everybody in the town.

Only, father's letters he keeps to read himself. I am sure the postman is a wicked man.
But don't be unhappy about that, mother dear.

Tomorrow is market day in the next village. You ask your maid to buy some pens and papers.
I myself will write all father's letters; you will not find a single mistake.
I shall write from A right up to K.

But, mother, why do you smile?
You don't believe that I can write as nicely as father does!

But I shall rule my paper carefully, and write all the letters beautifully big.
When I finish my writing, do you think I shall be so foolish as father and drop it into the horrid postman's bag?

I shall bring it to you myself without waiting, and letter by letter help you to read my writing.
I know the postman does not like to give you the really nice letters.

英 雄 /

媽媽，讓我們想像我們正在旅行，經過一個陌生而危
險的國土。
你坐在一頂轎子裡，我騎著一匹紅馬，在你旁邊跑著。
是黃昏的時候，太陽已經下山了。約拉地希的荒地疲
乏而灰暗地展開在我們面前。

大地是淒涼而荒蕪的。
你害怕了，想道 ──「我不知道我們到了什麼地方
了。」
我對你說道：「媽媽，不要害怕。」

草地上刺蓬蓬地長著針尖似的草，一條狹而崎嶇的小
道通過這塊草地。在這片廣大的地面上看不見一隻牛；
它們已經回到它們村裡的牛棚去了。

天色黑了下來，大地和天空都顯得朦朦朧朧的，而我
們不能說出我們正走向什麼所在。

突然間，你叫我，悄悄地問我道：「靠近河岸的是什
麼火光呀？」

正在那個時候，一陣可怕的吶喊聲爆發了，好些人影
子向我們跑過來。

你蹲坐在你的轎子裡，嘴裡反覆地禱念著神的名字。

轎夫們，怕得發抖，躲藏在荊棘叢中。

我向你喊道：「不要害怕，媽媽，有我在這裡。」

他們手裡執著長棒，頭髮披散著，越走越近了。

我喊道：「要當心！你們這些壞蛋！再向前走一步，
你們就要送命了。」

他們又發出一陣可怕的吶喊聲，向前衝過來。

你抓住我的手，說道：「好孩子，看在上天面上，躲開他們罷。」

我說道：「媽媽，你瞧我的。」

於是我刺策著我的馬匹，猛奔過去，我的劍和盾彼此碰著作響。

這一場戰鬥是那麼激烈，媽媽，如果你從轎子裡看得見的話，你一定會發冷戰的。

他們之中，許多人逃走了，還有好些人被砍殺了。

我知道你那時獨自坐在那裡，心裡正在想著，你的孩子這時候一定已經死了。

但是我跑到你的跟前，渾身濺滿了鮮血，說道：「媽媽，現在戰爭已經結束了。」

你從轎子裡走出來，吻著我，把我摟在你的心頭，你自言自語地說道：「如果我沒有我的孩子護送我，我簡直不知道怎麼辦才好。」

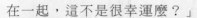

一千件無聊的事天天在發生，為什麼這樣一件事不能夠偶然實現呢？這很像一本書裡的一個故事。

我的哥哥要說道：「這是可能的事麼？我老是在想，他是那麼嫩弱呢！」

我們村裡的人都要驚訝地說道：「這孩子正和他媽媽在一起，這不是很幸運麼？」

The Hero /

Mother, let us imagine we are travelling, and passing through
a strange and dangerous country.
You are riding in a palanquin and I am trotting by you on a
red horse.
It is evening and the sun goes down. The waste of Joradighi
lies wan and grey before us.

The land is desolate and barren.
You are frightened and thinking — "I know not where we
have come to."
I say to you, "Mother, do not be afraid."

The meadow is prickly with spiky grass, and through it runs
a narrow broken path. There are no cattle to be seen in the
wide field; they have gone to their village stalls.

It grows dark and dim on the land and sky, and we cannot tell where we are going. Suddenly you call me and ask me in a whisper, "What light is that near the bank?"

Just then there bursts out a fearful yell, and figures come running towards us. You sit crouched in your palanquin and repeat the names of the gods in prayer.
The bearers, shaking in terror, hide themselves in the thorny bush.
I shout to you, "Don't be afraid, mother. I am here."

With long sticks in their hands and hair all wild about their heads, they come nearer and nearer.
I shout, "Have a care! you villains! One step more and you are dead men."

They give another terrible yell and rush forward.
You clutch my hand and say, "Dear boy, for heaven's sake, keep away from them."
I say, "Mother, just you watch me."

Then I spur my horse for a wild gallop, and my sword and buckler clash against each other.
The fight becomes so fearful, mother, that it would give you a cold shudder could you see it from your palanquin.

Many of them fly, and a great number are cut to pieces.
I know you are thinking, sitting all by yourself, that your boy must be dead by this time.

But I come to you all stained with blood, and say, "Mother, the fight is over now."

You come out and kiss me, pressing me to your heart, and you say to yourself, "I don't know what I should do if I hadn't my boy to escort me."

A thousand useless things happen day after day, and why couldn't such a thing come true by chance? It would be like a story in a book.

My brother would say, "Is it possible? I always thought he was so delicate!"

Our village people would all say in amazement, "Was it not lucky that the boy was with his mother?"

233

告 別 /

是我走的時候了，媽媽；我走了。

當清寂的黎明，你在暗中伸出雙臂，要抱你睡在床上的孩子時，我要說道：「孩子不在那裡呀！」—— 媽媽，我走了。

我要變成一股清風撫摸著你；我要變成水的漣漪，當你浴時，把你吻了又吻。

大風之夜，當雨點在樹葉中淅瀝時，你在床上，會聽見我的微語，當電光從開著的窗口閃進你的屋裡時，我的笑聲也偕了它一同閃進了。

如果你醒著躺在床上，想你的孩子到深夜，我便要從星空向你唱道：「睡呀！媽媽，睡呀。」

我要坐在各處遊蕩的月光上，偷偷地來到你的床上，乘你睡著時，躺在你的胸上。

我要變成一個夢，從你的眼皮的微縫中，鑽到你睡眠
的深處。當你醒來吃驚地四望時，我便如閃耀的螢火
似的熠熠地向暗中飛去了。

當普耶節日，鄰舍家的孩子來屋裡玩耍時，我便要融
化在笛聲裡，整日價在你心頭震盪。

親愛的阿姨帶了普耶禮來，問道：「我們的孩子在哪
裡，姊姊？」媽媽，你將要柔聲地告訴她：「他呀，
他現在是在我的瞳仁裡，他現在是在我的身體裡、在
我的靈魂裡。」

The End /

It is time for me to go, mother; I am going.
When in the paling darkness of the lonely dawn you stretch
out your arms for your baby in the bed, I shall say, "Baby is
not there!" — mother, I am going.

I shall become a delicate draught of air and caress you; and
I shall be ripples in the water when you bathe, and kiss you
and kiss you again.
In the gusty night when the rain patters on the leaves you
will hear my whisper in your bed, and my laughter will flash
with the lightning through the open window into your room.

If you lie awake, thinking of your baby till late into the night,
I shall sing to you from the stars, "Sleep mother, sleep."
On the straying moonbeams I shall steal over your bed, and
lie upon your bosom while you sleep.

I shall become a dream, and through the little opening of your eyelids I shall slip into the depths of your sleep, and when you wake up and look round startled, like a twinkling firefly I shall flit out into the darkness.

When, on the great festival of puja, the neighbours' children come and play about the house, I shall melt into the music of the flute and throb in your heart all day.

Dear auntie will come with puja-presents and will ask, "Where is our baby, sister?" Mother, you will tell her softly, "He is in the pupils of my eyes, he is in my body and in my soul."

召 喚 /

她走的時候，夜間黑漆漆的，他們都睡了。

現在，夜間也是黑漆漆的，我喚她道：「回來，我的寶貝；世界都在沉睡；當星星互相凝視的時候，你來一會兒是沒有人會知道的。」

她走的時候，樹木正在萌芽，春光剛剛來到。

現在花已盛開，我喚道：「回來，我的寶貝。孩子們漫不經心地在遊戲，把花聚在一起，又把它們散開。你如走來，拿一朵小花去，沒有人會發覺的。」

常常在遊戲的那些人，仍然還在那裡遊戲，生命總是如此地浪費。

我靜聽他們的空談，便喚道：「回來，我的寶貝，媽媽的心裡充滿著愛，你如走來，僅僅從她那裡接一個小小的吻，沒有人會妒忌的。」

The Recall /

The night was dark when she went away, and they slept.
The night is dark now, and I call for her, "Come back, my darling; the world is asleep; and no one would know, if you came for a moment while stars are gazing at stars."

She went away when the trees were in bud and the spring was young.
Now the flowers are in high bloom and I call, "Come back, my darling. The children gather and scatter flowers in reckless sport. And if you come and take one little blossom no one will miss it."

Those that used to play are playing still, so spendthrift is life.
I listen to their chatter and call, "Come back, my darling, for mother's heart is full to the brim with love, and if you come to snatch only one little kiss from her no one will grudge it."

第 一 次 的 茉 莉 /

呵，這些茉莉花，這些白的茉莉花！
我彷彿記得我第一次雙手滿捧著這些茉莉花，這些白
的茉莉花的時候。

我喜愛那日光，那天空，那綠色的大地；
我聽見那河水淙淙的流聲，在黑漆的午夜裡傳過來；
秋天的夕陽，在荒原上大路轉角處迎我，如新婦揭起
她的面紗迎接她的愛人。

但我想起孩提時第一次捧在手裡的白茉莉，心裡充滿
著甜蜜的回憶。
我生平有過許多快活的日子，在節日宴會的晚上，我
曾跟著說笑話的人大笑。

在灰暗的雨天的早晨，我吟哦過許多飄逸的詩篇。

我頸上戴過愛人手織的醉花的花圈，作為晚裝。

但我想起孩提時第一次捧在手裡的白茉莉，心裡充滿
著甜蜜的回憶。

The First Jasmines /

Ah, these jasmines, these white jasmines!
I seem to remember the first day when I filled my hands with
these jasmines, these white jasmines.

I have loved the sunlight, the sky and the green earth; I have
heard the liquid murmur of the river through the darkness of
midnight; Autumn sunsets have come to me at the bend of a
road in the lonely waste, like a bride raising her veil to accept
her lover.

Yet my memory is still sweet with the first white jasmines
that I held in my hand when I was a child.
Many a glad day has come in my life, and I have laughed
with merrymakers on festival nights.

On grey mornings of rain I have crooned many an idle song.
I have worn round my neck the evening wreath of bakulas
woven by the hand of love.
Yet my heart is sweet with the memory of the first fresh
jasmines that filled my hands when I was a child.

榕　樹 /

喂，你站在池邊的蓬頭的榕樹，你可會忘記了那小小的孩子，就像那在你的枝上築巢又離開了你的鳥兒似的孩子？
你不記得他是怎樣坐在窗內，詫異地望著你深入地下的糾纏的樹根麼？

婦人們常到池邊，汲了滿罐的水去，你的大黑影便在水面上搖動，好像睡著的人掙扎著要醒來似的。
日光在微波上跳舞，好像不停不息的小梭在織著金色的花氈。
兩隻鴨子挨著蘆葦，在蘆葦影子上游來游去，孩子靜靜地坐在那裡想著。

他想做風，吹過你的蕭蕭的枝杈；想做你的影子，在水面上，隨了日光而俱長；想做一隻鳥兒，棲息在你的最高枝上；還想做那兩隻鴨，在蘆葦與陰影中間游來游去。

The Banyan Tree /

O you shaggy-headed banyan tree standing on the bank of the pond, have you forgotten the little child, like the birds that have nested in your branches and left you?
Do you not remember how he sat at the window and wondered at the tangle of your roots that plunged underground?

The women would come to fill their jars in the pond, and your huge black shadow would wriggle on the water like sleep struggling to wake up.
Sunlight danced on the ripples like restless tiny shuttles weaving golden tapestry.
Two ducks swam by the weedy margin above their shadows, and the child would sit still and think.

He longed to be the wind and blow through your rustling branches, to be your shadow and lengthen with the day on the water, to be a bird and perch on your topmost twig, and to float like those ducks among the weeds and shadows.

祝 福 /

祝福這個小心靈，這個潔白的靈魂，他為我們的大地，贏得了天的接吻。
他愛日光，他愛見他媽媽的臉。
他沒有學會厭惡塵土而渴求黃金。
緊抱他在你的心裡，並且祝福他。

他已來到這個歧路百出的大地上了。
我不知道他怎麼從群眾中選出你來，來到你的門前抓住你的手問路。
他笑著，談著，跟著你走，心裡沒有一點兒疑惑。
不要辜負他的信任，引導他到正路，並且祝福他。

把你的手按在他的頭上，祈求著：底下的波濤雖然險惡，然而從上面來的風，會鼓起他的船帆，送他到和平的港口的。
不要在忙碌中把他忘了，讓他來到你的心裡，並且祝福他。

Benediction /

Bless this little heart, this white soul that has won the kiss of
heaven for our earth.
He loves the light of the sun, he loves the sight of his
mother's face.
He has not learned to despise the dust, and to hanker after
gold.
Clasp him to your heart and bless him.

He has come into this land of an hundred cross-roads.
I know not how he chose you from the crowd, came to your
door, and grasped your hand to ask his way.
He will follow you, laughing and talking, and not a doubt in
his heart.
Keep his trust, lead him straight and bless him.

Lay your hand on his head, and pray that though the waves
underneath grow threatening, yet the breath from above may
come and fill his sails and waft him to the haven of peace.
Forget him not in your hurry, let him come to your heart and
bless him.

禮 物 /

我要送些東西給你，我的孩子，因為我們同是漂泊在
世界的溪流中的。
我們的生命將被分開，我們的愛也將被忘記。
但我卻沒有那樣傻，希望能用我的禮物來買你的心。

你的生命正是青青，你的道路也長著呢，你一口氣飲
盡了我們帶給你的愛，便回身離開我們跑了。
你有你的遊戲，有你的遊伴。如果你沒有時間同我們
在一起，如果你想不到我們，那有什麼害處呢？

我們呢，自然的，在老年時，會有許多閒暇的時間，
去計算那過去的日子，把我們手裡永久失了的東西，
在心裡愛撫著。
河流唱著歌很快地流去，衝破所有的堤防。但是山峰
卻留在那裡，憶念著，滿懷依依之情。

The Gift /

I want to give you something, my child, for we are drifting in the stream of the world.
Our lives will be carried apart, and our love forgotten.
But I am not so foolish as to hope that I could buy your heart with my gifts.

Young is your life, your path long, and you drink the love we bring you at one draught and turn and run away from us.
You have your play and your playmates. What harm is there if you have no time or thought for us.

We, indeed, have leisure enough in old age to count the days that are past, to cherish in our hearts what our hands have lost for ever.
The river runs swift with a song, breaking through all barriers. But the mountain stays and remembers, and follows her with his love.

我 的 歌 /

我的孩子，我這一支歌將揚起它的樂聲圍繞你的身旁，
好像那愛情的熱戀的手臂一樣。
我這一支歌將觸著你的前額，好像那祝福的接吻一樣。

當你只是一個人的時候，它將坐在你的身旁，在你耳
邊微語著；當你在人群中的時候，它將圍住你，使你
超然物外。
我的歌將成為你的夢的翼翅，它將把你的心移送到不
可知的岸邊。

當黑夜覆蓋在你路上的時候，它又將成為那照臨在你
頭上的忠實的星光。我的歌又將坐在你眼睛的瞳仁裡，
將你的視線帶入萬物的心裡。
當我的聲音因死亡而沉寂時，我的歌仍將在你活潑潑
的心中唱著。

My Song /

This song of mine will wind its music around you, my child,
like the fond arms of love. This song of mine will touch your
forehead like a kiss of blessing.

When you are alone it will sit by your side and whisper in
your ear, when you are in the crowd it will fence you about
with aloofness.
My song will be like a pair of wings to your dreams, it will
transport your heart to the verge of the unknown.

It will be like the faithful star overhead when dark night is
over your road.
My song will sit in the pupils of your eyes, and will carry
your sight into the heart of things.
And when my voice is silent in death, my song will speak in
your living heart.

孩 子 的 天 使 /

他們喧嘩爭鬥，他們懷疑失望，他們辯論而沒有結果。
我的孩子，讓你的生命到他們當中去，如一線鎮定而
純潔之光，使他們愉悅而沉默。

他們的貪心和妒忌是殘忍的；他們的話，好像暗藏的
刀，渴欲飲血。
我的孩子，去，去站在他們憤懣的心中，把你的和善
的眼光落在他們上面，好像那傍晚的寬宏大量的和平，
覆蓋著日間的騷擾一樣。

我的孩子，讓他們望著你的臉，因此能夠知道一切事
物的意義；讓他們愛你，因此他們能夠相愛。

來，坐在無垠的胸膛上，我的孩子。朝陽出來時，開
放而且抬起你的心，像一朵盛開的花；夕陽落下時，
低下你的頭，默默地做完這一天的禮拜。

The Child-angel /

They clamour and fight, they doubt and despair, they know no end to their wranglings.
Let your life come amongst them like a flame of light, my child, unflickering and pure, and delight them into silence.

They are cruel in their greed and their envy, their words are like hidden knives thirsting for blood.
Go and stand amidst their scowling hearts, my child, and let your gentle eyes fall upon them like the forgiving peace of the evening over the strife of the day.

Let them see your face, my child, and thus know the meaning of all things; let them love you and thus love each other.

Come and take your seat in the bosom of the limitless, my child. At sunrise open and raise your heart like a blossoming flower, and at sunset bend your head and in silence complete the worship of the day.

最 後 的 買 賣 /

早晨，我在石鋪的路上走時，我叫道：「誰來雇用我
呀。」
皇帝坐著馬車，手裡拿著劍走來。
他拉著我的手，說道：「我要用權力來雇用你。」
但是他的權力算不了什麼，他坐著馬車走了。

正午炎熱的時候，家家戶戶的門都閉著。
我沿著彎曲的小巷走去。一個老人帶著一袋金錢走出
來。
他斟酌了一下，說道：「我要用金錢來雇用你。」
他一個一個地數著他的錢，我卻轉身離去了。

黃昏了，花園的籬上滿開著花。

美人走出來，說道：「我要用微笑來雇用你。」

她的微笑黯淡了，化成淚容了，她孤寂地回身走進黑暗裡去。

太陽照耀在沙地上，海波任性地浪花四濺。

一個小孩坐在那裡玩貝殼。

他抬起頭來，好像認識我似的，說道：「我雇你不用什麼東西。」

從此以後，在這個小孩的遊戲中做成的買賣，使我成了一個自由的人。

The Last Bargain /

"Come and hire me," I cried, while in the morning I was walking on the stone-paved road.
Sword in hand, the King came in his chariot.
He held my hand and said, "I will hire you with my power."
But his power counted for nought, and he went away in his chariot.

In the heat of the midday the houses stood with shut doors.
I wandered along the crooked lane.
An old man came out with his bag of gold.
He pondered and said, "I will hire you with my money."
He weighed his coins one by one, but I turned away.

It was evening. The garden hedge was all a flower.

The fair maid came out and said, "I will hire you with a smile."

Her smile paled and melted into tears, and she went back alone into the dark.

The sun glistened on the sand, and the sea waves broke waywardly.

A child sat playing with shells.

He raised his head and seemed to know me, and said, "I hire you with nothing."

From thenceforward that bargain struck in child's play made me a free man.

「這冊《太戈爾傳》原登載於一九二三年九月及十月號《小說月報》上。單行本本想在太戈爾到中國時出版。不料擱置於印刷的地方直到了現在。因為近來很忙，不能再細讀一過，所以除了一二小錯誤曾改正了之外，其餘文字一概都照舊。」

——鄭振鐸

附錄

《太戈爾傳》 [1]

　　拉賓德拉納特‧太戈爾是現代印度的一個最偉大的詩人，也是現代世界的一個最偉大的詩人。

　　他的作品，加入彭加爾 [2]（Bengal）文學內，如注生命汁給垂死的人似的，立刻使彭加爾的文學成了一種新的學；他清新流麗的譯文，加入英國的文學裡，也如在萬紫千紅的園林中，突現了一株翠綠的熱帶長青樹似的，立刻樹立了一種特異的新穎文體。

　　現代詩人的情思，對於我們似乎都太熟悉了；我們聽熟了他們的歌聲，我們讀熟了他們的情語，我們知道他們一切所要說的話，我們知道他們一切所要敘述的方法，他們的聲音，已不能再引起我們的注意了。太戈爾之加入世界的文壇，正在這個舊的一切，已為我們厭倦的時候。他的特異的祈禱，他的創造的新聲，他的甜蜜的戀歌，一切都如清晨的曙光，照耀著我們久居黑暗長夜中的人的眼前。

---

1 本文節選自鄭振鐸：《太戈爾傳》，商務印書館，一九二五年。
2 彭加爾即孟加拉。

這就是他所以能這樣的使我們注意、這樣的使我們歡迎的最大原因。

他同時又是一個偉大的哲學家;他的哲學思想,也如他的詩歌和其他作品一樣,能跳出近代的一切爭辯與陳腐的空氣,而自創一個新的局面。

他在舉世膜拜西方的物質文明的時候,獨振盪他的銀鈴似的歌聲,歌頌東方的森林的文化。他的勇氣實是不能企及。

我們對於現代的這樣一個偉大人物似乎至少應該有些瞭解。

他現在是快要到中國來了,我且乘這個機會,在此敘述他的生平大略,以作為大家瞭解他的一個小幫助。

他的傳記本身也是一篇美麗的敘事詩。印度人都讚羨著他完美的生活。自他的童年以至現在,他幾乎無一天不在詩化的國土裡生活著。我們讀他的傳記正如讀一篇好詩,沒有不深深受它的感動的。我所以要介紹他的傳記,這也是一個小原因。

一、家世

太戈爾生於一八六一年五月六日。他的生地是印度的彭加爾地方。

印度是一個「詩的國」。詩就是印度人日常生活的一部分。新生的兒童到了這個世界上所受的第一次祝福,就是用韻文唱的。孩子大了如做了不好的事，他母親必定背誦一首小詩告訴他這種行為的不對。在初等學校裡，教了字母之後，學生所受的第一課書就是一首詩。許多青年的心裡所受的最初的教訓就是：「兩個偉大的祝福，能消除這個艱苦的世界的恐怖的，就是嘗詩的甘露與交好的朋友。」許多印度人做的書也都用詩的形式來寫；文法的條規，數學的法則，乃至博物學、醫學、天文學、化學、物理學，都是如此。結婚的時候，唱的是歡愉之詩；死屍火葬的時候，他們最後對死人說的話，也是引用印度的詩篇。在這個「詩之國」裡，產生了這個偉大的詩人太戈爾，自然是沒有什麼奇怪的。他的家庭是印度的著名望族。近百年來，這個家庭的搖籃裡繼續產生了不少偉大的人物，為彭加爾地方的文藝復興的先驅者。無論在社會與宗教的改革、在藝術與音樂的復興、在政治與實業的組織上，他們都立有很大的功績。所以印度的人民，尤其是彭加爾的人民，一講起這個家族都帶著十二分的敬意。在這樣的家庭產生了他，也是沒有什麼奇怪的。

二、童年時代

　　大詩人的太戈爾在這樣的一個家庭中度過他的童年。

　　他和別的兩個孩子一起讀書，他們都比他大兩歲；那時所讀的東西，他早已忘懷；他所記得最真切的只有：「雨濺葉顫」及「雨淅瀝地落下，潮水泛溢到河上來」兩句。這是他與文學第一次的接觸；他說，當時的印象，到現在還沒有消滅。

他在家中，不常見到他父親；那個「大哲」是常在外面旅行的。他幼年的保護者是幾個男僕人，他們都是很粗心很自私的。他們常常為免除他們的看護的麻煩起見，把小孩子關在一間屋裡，不准他們自由行動。有一個僕人，常叫太戈爾坐在一個指定的地點，用粉筆在地上畫了一個圓圈，把他包圍起來，並且驚嚇他說，如果他離開這個圓圈一步，就會有危險。他便坐在那裡動也不動。因為他讀過《拉摩耶那》（Ramayana），知道有一個人因為擅自離開別人所畫的圈子，後來竟遇到許多危險。

幸而他所坐的地方，常近於窗口：他從窗中能夠看見花園，看見一個池、許多行樹，還看著往來的人與鳥兒等；鴨子在池中游泳，樹影在水面映動。有一株榕樹，尤使他注意，他在後來曾有一首詩寫到它。

「呵，古老的榕樹，你的絞繞的樹根從枝上掛下來，你日夜站著不動，如一個修道者之在懺悔，你還記得那個孩子，他的幻想曾隨了你的陰影，而遊戲的嗎？」

天然的景色，使他忘了囚禁之苦。

三、浪漫的少年時代

太戈爾現在是一個十八歲的少年；他飲著青春的酒，他的熱情，他的感觸，奔馳而外放，他所見的僅是愛情與浪漫。同樣的自然、同樣的人民、同樣的生活，然而現在對於他似乎都變了一個樣子。他要知道，這是他自己變了呢，還是世界變了呢？不久，他便發現，他自己是先變，然後與他接觸的世界也變了。他童年時代的神祕主義已經還給了森林與花與山與星。他現在已不是一個神祕者而是一個寫實主義者了，有一個時期，他竟成了一個享樂主義者，──穿著最好的時式的絲裳，吃著美食，作著敘愛情的抒情詩及其他文藝作品。

他和他家裡的人，這時似乎都很隔膜。他在五十歲時，自己曾說道，「我自十六歲至二十三歲的一個時期的生活是一個極端的放浪與不守規則的生活。」但他這時所作的抒情詩，卻都是極好的詩。

「我跑著，如香麝之在林影中跑，聞著他自己的芳香而發狂。

夜是五月的夜，風是南來的風，我迷了路，我浪遊著，我尋求我所不能得到的東西，我得到我所不尋求的東西。我自己欲望的印象從我心裡跑出來，在跳著舞。

熠耀的幻象閃過去。

我想把它緊緊的握住，它避開我，引我到

迷路。

　　我尋求我所不能得到的東西，我得到我所
不尋求的東西。」

太戈爾在這時候，正是「聞著他自己的芳香而
發狂」的時候。他在〈快樂的悲哀〉裡又寫道，「快
樂睜開他的倦眼，長長的歎了一口氣，說道：『我
在這樣的一個明月滿地的夜裡，僅有孤零零的一個
人。』於是所有他的思想，都放在歌聲中——我是
怕孤寂的，我不見一個人來拜訪我——我是孤獨的，
我是孤獨的。」

四、變遷時代

太戈爾的浪漫的少年生活，到了二十三歲時告
了終止。他這時候正與一個女子結了婚。靈的感覺，
漸漸的在心裡占了優勢，他漸漸的捨棄了他清新的
戀歌調子，而從事於神的讚頌。可愛的神，已把他
的面紗卸下了。

　　「清晨的時候，我在自由學校街上看日出。
一層紗幕放開了，我所見一切的東西都清明起
來。全部的景色是一部完美的音樂，一部神奇
的韻律。街上的屋宇，兒童的遊戲，一切都似
是一個明澈的全體的一部分——不能表達的絢
麗。這個幻景繼續了七八天。每個人，即那些

吵擾我的人，也都似失掉他們人格的外層牆界；我是充滿了快樂，充滿了愛，對於每一個人及每一最微小的東西……在自由學校街上的那天清晨是第一次給我以內在的幻景的事物之一，我想把它表白在我的詩裡。從那時候起，我覺得這就是我生活的鵠的：表白出人生的充實，在它的美麗裡，證明其為完整的。」

這就是他看見放下面紗後的神或自然的經過。

在這一天，他作了一首詩，名為：〈泉的覺醒〉，這首詩在藝術上雖不能算是極高，卻足以極表現出太戈爾那時的內在的情緒與他的個性。

「我不知我的生命經歷了這許多年以後，到今天怎麼還會有這樣的一種覺醒。我也不知道，在清晨的時候，太陽的真光怎麼會射進我的心，或那晨鳥的音樂怎麼會鑽入我心房的黑暗的最深處。

現在，我的全心身是覺醒了。我不能制馭我心的願望。看呀！全個世界連基礎都顫震著，峰與山紛亂的卓列著；帶著水沫的波浪在憤怒的洶湧著，似乎要撕裂這個地球的心，以報禁制它自由的仇怨。大海受了朝陽之光的接觸，表現著喧嘩的狂樂，意欲吞沒世界以求它自己的充滿。

呵，殘酷的上帝！為什麼你把大海也禁制住了？」

五、和平之院

　　太戈爾在一九〇七年時，即與實際的政治與政治運動斷絕關係。遠在這個時候以前，他的內心裡，感到一種變遷的光，這個變遷要求因印度的再造而為更完滿的犧牲。他不注意政治、經濟及其他，而欲用教育的改造為印度改造的基礎。充滿了自由與愛的教育不僅能發展智力與道德，而且能造成一個精神的人。他最反對強迫的注入式教育；他以為教育的全步程，應該愈簡易愈自然愈好，務使兒童受最少的痛苦。為要實現他的主張，他便在鮑爾甫[3]（Bolpur）辦了一個學校。校址即為以前他的父親用來靜修的「和平之院」（Shantineketan）。經濟與社會的批評，常成為他的計畫的阻礙。但他的父親卻很幫助他。他的精神也極堅定，絕不因外界的影響而自餒。一九四二年，這個學校便開始成立。最初僅有三、四個學生。太戈爾自己的兒子是第一個入學的人。他自己有關於這個學校的一段話：

　　「我為了要再現我們古代教育制度的精神，決定創辦一個學校，學生在那裡能夠在生命裡感覺到一個比現實的滿足更高尚更光榮的東西——熟悉生命它自己。我想把小孩子們的奢侈除去，使他們復返於樸質。所以因此之故，我們的學校裡，沒有班次，也沒有凳子。我們的小孩子，在樹下鋪了席子，在那裡讀書；他們的生活，力求其簡單。這個學校建立在大平原裡的大原因之一，即在於要遠遠地離開了城市生活，但在這一層以外，我更要看孩子們與樹木一同生長；因此兩者的生長之中有了一種和諧。在城市裡看不見什麼樹。他們是為城牆所限禁的。城牆不會生長，石塊與磚頭的死重壓抑了兒童天性裡的自然的快樂。

我在學校裡，並不曾得到最好一類的孩子。社會看這個學校為一個刑罰的住所。大部分的學生都是因父親不能管束，才把他們送到這裡來。」

六、得諾貝爾獎金與其後

一九一三年的冬天，瑞典的文學會，以諾貝爾獎金（Nobel Prize）奉給太戈爾。這是東方人第一次在歐洲得到的榮譽。在這個時候以前，太戈爾的《吉檀迦利》（Gitanjali）的出版，雖然使歐洲讀它的人為之驚異不置，然而對於太戈爾並未十分瞭解。但從這個把一九一三年的諾貝爾獎金給予他的消息

---

3 鮑爾甫即波浦爾。

傳出後，他的名字才常常在許多平常人的口中說著，他的作品才常常有人去研究，他的思想和生平，才常常有人想要知道。他的文學上的地位，從這時起才在世界文壇上確定了；他的名譽，也從這時起才變為世界的了——不僅歐洲人、美洲人，知道他，連東方的中國與日本向來與世界文學，尤其是自己東方的近代文學，不相接近的，也立刻認識了他。

　　這一次諾貝爾文學獎金之給予太戈爾，除了關於太戈爾的自身外，許多人都以為是世界上一個很大的消息。歐洲的文壇，本來不大與東方的文壇接近，對於近代東方文學尤有蔑視之意。從這時以後，這種意見才漸漸的泯滅。一個美國的著作家說道：「這個獎金將勉勵西方的人類去訪求東方的人類所已說的話，或將要說的話。這件事將把以前永未解釋過的東方，為西方解釋一下。所以這件事成了一件歷史上的事實，一個那半球明白這半球的轉點。」不僅如此，這件事且表白出東與西的友誼、一個新時代的黎明。東與西的文學，藝術與理想的互相瞭解、互相讚賞，如一陣大風似的，能夠把國際間或人種間的敵視與歧異的見解的黑雲吹散到天外去。這個期望，我們在這時說出，也許覺得是過早，但我們看太戈爾近來在歐洲的影響與他近來的努力的成績，卻使我們絕不能相信這是一種不可能的期望。

關於太戈爾研究的書：

(1) 《太戈爾與其詩》，洛依著。

(R. Tagore：The Man and His Poetry. by B. K. Roy)

(2) 《太戈爾傳》，里斯著。

(R. Tagore：A. Biographical Study. by Ernest Rhys)

(3) 《太戈爾的哲學》，拉哈克里希南著。

(The Philosophy of R. Tagore. by S. Radhaklrishnan)

(4)《山底尼克頓》，批爾孫著（此書述太氏創辦的「和平之院」之事）。

(Shantiniketan. by Pearsen)

譯者簡介

鄭振鐸
（1898 — 1958）

　　中國現代作家、文學評論家、文學史家、藝術史家，曾歷任清華大學、燕京大學、輔仁大學教授與暨南大學文學院院長，《世界文庫》主編。主要著作有短篇小説集《家庭的故事》、《桂公塘》，散文集《山中雜記》，專著《文學大綱》、《插圖本中國文學史》、《中國俗文學史》等。由他傾心翻譯的泰戈爾《新月集》、《飛鳥集》，被世人公認為經典譯本。